For the first time, natural, spectacular smile. In the glow from the porch light, her long auburn hair glistened and her green eyes shimmered. Her lips parted, showing off a row of perfect white teeth.

Jake swallowed hard and forced himself to speak coherently. "I'll get the surveillance underway."

"Good work, Jake."

This might be the first time she'd used his given name. He'd graduated from the generic *detective* or *Armstrong.* "Thank you, Skylar."

Leaning into the shadows on the porch, she wrapped her arms around his torso for a hug. Her slender body pressed against his chest. He draped his arms over her shoulders and gently squeezed, imagining the sound of their hearts beating in harmony.

Their brief contact—probably less than five seconds—wasn't strictly professional, but he'd forgotten about his image and credibility. His mind filled with images of further intimacy. Maybe a kiss. Maybe more.

He wanted Skylar beside him in his bed.

THE
LIGHTKEEPER'S
CURSE

CASSIE MILES

Harlequin

INTRIGUE

Thanks to Julie Drey, an author who can really
sling a curse. And, as always, to Rick.

Harlequin®
INTRIGUE™

ISBN-13: 978-1-335-45737-0

The Lightkeeper's Curse

Copyright © 2025 by Kay Bergstrom

Recycling programs
for this product may
not exist in your area.

Harlequin Enterprises ULC
22 Adelaide St. West, 41st Floor
Toronto, Ontario M5H 4E3, Canada
www.Harlequin.com

Printed in Lithuania

MIX
Paper | Supporting
responsible forestry
FSC® C021394

Cassie Miles, a *USA TODAY* bestselling author, lived in Colorado for many years and has now moved to Oregon. Her home is an hour from the rugged Pacific Ocean and an hour from the Cascade Mountains—the best of both worlds—not to mention the incredible restaurants in Portland and award-winning wineries in the Willamette Valley. She's looking forward to exploring the Pacific Northwest and finding mysterious new settings for Harlequin Intrigue romances.

Books by Cassie Miles

Harlequin Intrigue

Lighthouse Mysteries

Fugitive Harbor
The Lightkeeper's Curse

K-9 Hunter
Shallow Grave
Escape from Ice Mountain
Gaslighted in Colorado
Find Me
Cold Case Colorado
Witness on the Run
The Final Secret
The Girl Who Couldn't Forget
The Girl Who Wouldn't Stay Dead
Frozen Memories
Mountain Blizzard
Mountain Shelter
Mountain Bodyguard
Colorado Wildfire
Mountain Retreat

Visit the Author Profile page at Harlequin.com.

CAST OF CHARACTERS

Skylar Gambel—The FBI special agent, newly assigned to Oregon, eagerly starts her first active investigation after a career in research and law. She has a phobia of bridges.

Jake Armstrong—The former marine is a detective in the Astoria Police Department (APD) with a personal connection to the Lightkeeper Murders from twenty years ago.

Phoebe Conway, Lucille Dixon and Portia—Victims of the Shadowkeeper.

Dagmar Burke—Her mother was the last victim of the Lightkeeper.

Chief Vivienne Kim—The pregnant APD police chief.

Joseph Rogers—Editor in chief of the *Astoria Sun*.

Bradley Rogers—Son of Joseph who was terrorized as a child by the Lightkeeper.

Alan Quilling—A forensic specialist implicated by evidence from a traffic cam.

Ty McKenna—The hipster reporter considers himself a ladies' man.

Robert (Pyro) Pierce—Dagmar's boyfriend is a science teacher with ties to a victim.

Hear me, o goddesses,
West, East, North, South.
Scratch out his eyes.
Muzzle his mouth.

Bind his arms.
Heed not his plea.
Death to the Keeper.
So mote it be.

Chapter One

Heavy clouds obscured the moonlight and stars above Cape Meares, west of Tillamook Bay on the Oregon shoreline. Through the darkness, Phoebe Conway crept through tendrils of fog weaving through spruce, hemlock and rugged coastal pines. Her instincts told her to turn around and dash back to her car parked at the scenic viewpoint off Highway 101, but life was about more than mere survival.

She had gold-plated ambition. Whatever happened tonight could be her big break. The instructions told her to come at midnight to the Cape Meares Lighthouse and to come alone. She was willing to take the risk.

Earlier today, a plain white envelope with no return address appeared on her desk at the *Astoria Sun* newspaper. Nobody saw the person who dropped the note with her name in bold above the newspaper's address. She'd read and reread:

I have new evidence about the Lightkeeper's Curse Murders. You should be the reporter to tell this story, Phoebe. You're a shining star from the Lone Star state but unappreciated. I'll make sure you get what you deserve. Tell no one about this contact. Don't bring a phone or a camera. Cape Meares Lighthouse at midnight.

She wished there had been a signature or an email address—some way to verify the identity of the person who wrote the note. Was it someone who'd been alive in the early 2000s when the serial murders took place? Or a descendant of the Lightkeeper killer? Perhaps the Lightkeeper himself? After all, he'd never been arrested.

Maybe he'd been waiting all this time for the right reporter to come along—waiting for her. The article she'd written about *The Goonies*, a classic movie filmed in Astoria, had been picked up by several major newspapers and had led to three television appearances on the local news in Portland and Seattle. In her vintage letterman's sweater and short white skirt suggesting the costume worn by the female lead, Phoebe had looked fantastic. Camera-ready. Meant to be a star.

If this mysterious note-writer had new information about the infamous Lightkeeper's Curse, she might have the scoop of the century.

Shivering in the October chill, she flipped up the collar on her jacket and followed the downward sloping asphalt path from the parking lot to the lighthouse. A rough wooden railing bordered the seaward side where the trees were spread far enough apart for her to glimpse the churning waves of the Pacific.

The screech of a nighthawk startled her, and she waved her flashlight to chase the bird away. The beam reflected off the fog, giving substance to the wispy shapes. The mossy tree branches looked like claws reaching toward her, trying to grab her blond ponytail and drag her down, down, down. The fog took on terrifying shapes. A humpback monster. A dragon. A ghoul.

She heard a sound behind her and whipped around, dancing on the toes of her sneakers. "Who's there?"

Nothing but darkness and a shredded curtain of mist. The wind droned through the boughs and branches of the nearby wilderness preserve in an eerie hum.

Did she hear an undercurrent of laughter? Again, she pivoted. Her flashlight beam wavered madly. Her pulse raced. She clenched her jaw and marched onward. This was no time to be scared of the dark.

She rounded the last curve and approached the octagonal, whitewashed brick lighthouse that stood on a rocky promontory at the edge of a two-hundred-foot cliff.

Not a particularly impressive structure, the decommissioned lighthouse was the shortest in Oregon. Only thirty-eight feet high but beautifully maintained by the Park Service, the tower and attached gift shop opened every day from morning until dusk. A porch light hung over the door to the shop, but the bulb must have burned out. Shifting glimmers of moonlight provided the only illumination.

A bit of online research told her the red-and-white flashing Fresnel beacon—when operational—had been visible from twenty-one nautical miles away. Starting in the early 1890s, the Cape Meares Lighthouse guided sailors through the treacherous rocks, shoals and sandbars on the coastal route from southern California to British Columbia. These fraught seas caused an estimated three thousand shipwrecks, including the rusted skeleton of a hull she'd visited on a stretch of beach and a cannon that washed ashore near Haystack Rock.

She stood at the wooden railing, watching the fog and the endless ocean. In the rumble of the surf, she heard echoes of lost souls—the dying screams from sailors calling for help that never came.

Some people saw lighthouses as symbols of hope. Too often, hope wasn't enough.

Phoebe turned her back on the sea and studied the squat tower that stood before her. Where the hell was her mysterious informant? The night was too cold to play games, and she felt the first splash of a raindrop on her forehead.

"Hello?" she called out. "It's me. Phoebe."

No human voice responded. Only the whisper from the

wind and the rattle of the surf. Though she appreciated the drama of the ominous setting, which would play well when she wrote her article, enough was enough. "Okay, whoever you are. Show yourself."

"Here."

The deep voice shocked her, and she looked in the direction it seemed to come from. Upward. A person in a black hoodie stood on the circular balcony wrapped around the tower at the same level as the beacon.

Darkness and fog shrouded the figure, but Phoebe had the impression that he was big. "Who are you? Can you give me your name?"

A long arm beckoned to her. "Come."

She hesitated. Something in his voice scared her. They were out here alone. Her hand slipped into her shoulder bag before she remembered that she'd obeyed the note and left her work phone at her office at the *Sun*. Her personal phone was in her car, leaving her unable to call 911.

The figure turned away from her.

"Wait," she called after him. "I did everything you asked." Not one hundred percent true. Though she hadn't spoken to anyone, she'd used her work phone to take a picture of the note he'd delivered. Since he hadn't specifically mentioned weapons, she'd armed herself with a stun gun. If he attacked her, twenty-five thousand volts ought to be enough to slow him down.

He disappeared into the tower.

Reaching into her the pocket of her jacket, she wrapped her fingers around the handle of the stun gun while holding her flashlight with the other hand. She shouted, "I'm coming. Don't leave. I want to hear your story."

She circled around to the gift shop—a small, attached house that had once been used by crews who tended the beacon. The door was unlocked, and she stepped inside just as the raindrops turned into a storm that would turn her long blond hair into a frizzled mess.

The shop displayed books, T-shirts, postcards and tourist junk. Behind the counter with the cash register stood a row of three-foot-tall replicas of the Cape Meares Lighthouse. Their rotating beacons provided the only light in the shop. The flashes disconcerted her. She blinked and turned away. But then she moved forward. One step at a time.

She left the door ajar so she could make a speedy exit if need be.

When she crossed the shop and entered the actual tower, her gaze traveled around the whitewashed wall to an elegant wrought iron staircase that molded to the octagonal shape of the walls. The glow from moon and stars shone through a narrow window and from the top of the stair. A faint and eerie illumination. Was he up at the top, waiting for her?

She cleared her throat and put some force into her voice. "Hello. Are you here?"

The door to the gift shop slammed. She turned and saw a hooded figure coming at her, vaulting through the racks of T-shirts and shelves of knickknacks.

She froze, unable to believe her eyes. He couldn't have gotten down from the upper level and outside so quickly. "How did you get past me?"

"Climbed down from the outside." He came closer.

"Stay back."

Lightning fast, he grasped her wrists and twisted her arms behind her. Both the stun gun and the flashlight crashed to the floor. Handcuffs clicked into place.

Roughly, he shoved her around to face him. The lower half of his face was masked, but she recognized him immediately.

"I promised new information," he growled. "Here's your scoop, Phoebe."

"Let me go. I don't care."

"There will be more murders to come. Starting with yours."

She heard herself scream. And knew that no one would be coming to her rescue.

Chapter Two

Special Agent Skylar Gambel had paid her dues. After two years working with the prosecuting attorney's office in her hometown of San Francisco, graduation with honors from the FBI Academy in Quantico and four years of desk work as an analyst at the J. Edgar Hoover Building in DC, she had transferred to the Portland FBI field office where she gladly took on the responsibilities of a special agent. Mentally, she underlined *gladly*. It felt like she'd been waiting all her life for this opportunity to be an active investigator.

In addition to her thorough training and education, she had great instincts. Her first impressions of people were nearly as accurate as a computer profile or a lie detector. Ninety-seven times out of a hundred, she could pick the criminal from a lineup. Not a particularly desirable ability for an attorney who ought to presume innocence, even as a prosecutor.

Always look on the bright side of life, right? She struggled to keep an open mind, even when she intuited the truth.

By the end of her third week in Oregon, she felt settled in her new city. Portland offered gourmet dining, fantastic coffee shops, artsy events and Powell's, which was supposed to be the largest independent bookstore in the world. She'd joined a fantastic dojo to practice her karate skills and take new instruction in Krav Maga. She varied the route for her morning run to check out the local gardens, waterfalls and forests.

As far as she was concerned, the only real negative to living in Portland was…bridges. Getting around town almost always meant traversing one or two or more overpasses. Not her favorite thing. She hated the way the prestressed concrete shuddered beneath her tires or the indefinable but frightening sense of dangling in midair. Crossing over rivers and waterways always sparked a twinge of vertigo. A knot in the gut. Accelerated pulse rate. Her reaction was similar to a panic attack.

If she concentrated, she could keep her nasty little phobia under control. If not, she might have a real meltdown. Not a good look for an FBI special agent.

Before lunch on Thursday, she got an important, interesting assignment: an active murder investigation in Astoria at the mouth of the Columbia River. *Finally!*

Though eager to get started, she curbed her enthusiasm. Celebration would be grossly inappropriate, given the gruesome nature of the crime. The victim—twenty-nine years old, the same age as Skylar—died from manual strangulation at the historic lighthouse on Cape Meares.

Though tours of the lighthouse and gift shop ended in September, a Park Service ranger on his morning rounds at the scenic viewpoint noticed the door to the gift shop was open. Inside, he discovered the victim's lifeless body gracefully arranged on the swooping staircase leading to the lighthouse beacon. She'd been blindfolded and gagged with her wrists handcuffed behind her back.

Standing at her desk, Skylar looked over the case notes and the crime scene photos displayed on her computer. The long legs of the dead woman were tucked demurely beneath her on a lower step of the black, wrought iron stairs. Her torso leaned against the railing. Her long blond hair draped across her face, held in place by the bandanna tied over her eyes. A square of duct tape covered her mouth. The dark bruise on her throat could barely be seen under her neatly combed and styled hair, an indication that she hadn't been outside last night in the rain. Also, her sneakers didn't appear to be muddy.

In her work as an analyst, Skylar had seen her share of crime scene photos. Many captured a sense of the untimely death, as if the victim had been interrupted or surprised in the middle of doing something else. Their life was cut short. Expectations erased. That was surely the case with Phoebe Conway, a successful reporter at the *Astoria Sun* newspaper, who had been identified at the scene using the driver's license from her wallet.

Skylar silently promised Phoebe that her killer would be brought to justice. That was her job as a special agent. With a renewed sense of purpose, she holstered her Glock 19 under the jacket of her charcoal gray suit before turning toward her partner. "I'm ready."

The handsome, white-haired senior agent named Harold Crawford—often referred to around the office as the Silver Fox—acted as her supervisor and mentor. He reached into the lower left drawer in his desk, took out a battered nine-by-twelve envelope and dropped it with a thud on his desktop beside the framed photo of his three grandchildren. "First, we're going to Astoria."

"Not the crime scene at Cape Meares?"

"Astoria," he repeated. "Do you have a change of clothes?"

"In my locker." She tucked a strand of dark auburn hair into the low ponytail at her nape and straightened the light blue collar of her blouse.

"We'll be doing some hiking." He stared pointedly at her shoes.

"I'm prepared." Of course, she had alternate footwear. "Unless there's some kind of special dress code for Astoria."

"Don't be a smart-ass. My wife thinks you look and dress

like a recruitment poster for professional women in the FBI, but you're just another newbie in my book."

Growing up with two older brothers had prepared her for teasing. Crawford was like a favorite uncle with a pseudo-grumpy sense of humor. "The boss mentioned that you have a history with this investigation," she said. "The Lightkeeper's Curse Murders?"

His forehead pinched into a frown. "We'll talk on the way. Astoria is about a hundred miles from here, and the ride takes two or two-and-a-half hours, which means we'll get there around three. I asked you about clothes because we'll stay overnight."

"No problem." In addition to the go bag in her locker, she had more clothes, equipment and her bulletproof vest in the trunk of her car, all of which she transferred to the fleet vehicle they signed out for the trip.

Within forty-five minutes of getting their assignment, she and Crawford hit the road in an unmarked black Chevy Suburban. While he navigated Portland traffic and merged onto Route 30 headed northwest toward the coast, she studied printouts of police reports she'd tucked into the extra-large briefcase on the floor between her feet, clad in sensible boots.

The body of Phoebe Conway was found this morning at about half-past nine. The Oregon Park Service employee notified the Tillamook County sheriff's office, who established a crime scene, contacted the coroner and arranged for the deceased to be taken to the Clatsop County medical examiner. They advised them to contact the police chief in Astoria who, in turn, reached out to the Portland FBI field office.

She glanced over at Crawford. "Jurisdiction on this murder has been bouncing around like a pinball. Right now, it looks like the ME in Warrenton passed the ball to the police chief in Astoria."

"Correct. That would be Chief Vivienne Kim. The veteran ME is Dr. Kate Kinski. I'll recommend that she do the autopsy instead of shipping the remains to Portland."

"Tell me why the FBI is involved."

"I might have pulled a few strings," he admitted.

"Because of the serial murders that happened over twenty years ago?"

While keeping his eye on the road, he nodded slowly. "The Lightkeeper Murders. Seven women were killed. All their bodies were found at or near lighthouses in Clatsop County, Tillamook County and across the Columbia River in Washington state at Cape Disappointment."

Cape Disappointment? Well, that's a colorful name. She drew the obvious conclusion. "We were consulted due to the multijurisdictional nature."

"Partially," he said. "Twenty years ago, I was part of the task force. You'll find details in the envelope I took from my desk. I already stuck it into your briefcase."

She dug through the files and found the worn, tattered envelope. Since he still kept that cold case evidence close at hand, she figured SSA Crawford hadn't given up on solving the murders. "Never caught the guy?"

"Never did."

The envelope held extensive reports, depositions, photos and whatever. Digging through it was daunting. "Instead of reading," she said, "I'd rather hear the story from you."

"Straight from the horse's mouth?"

"Talk to me, Seabiscuit."

She leaned back in the passenger seat and prepared to listen. In the distance, she saw the truncated peak of Mount St. Helens across the river in Washington. The snow-covered summit of Mount Hood was in the rearview mirror, still visible in the midafternoon sunlight of a clear autumn day.

In addition to bridges, Oregon was all about trees. Amid conifers, spruce, cedars and pines, a hundred different shades of green surrounded her, starting with the blackberry and chokecherry thickets close to the ground and rising past vines, ferns and boughs to the towering spires of Sitka spruce. The gold and scarlet of autumn appeared in the aspens, larches and maples. Beautiful. Peaceful. Wild.

And dangerous. Wildfires had blackened many of the formerly verdant hillsides, leaving jagged tree stumps and stacks of scrap wood. The skeletons of a small enclave— three dwellings, a garage, outbuildings, fence and a one-story horse barn—spoke of destruction and devastation. The serenity of the forests masked a darker reality.

Crawford continued to speak in a calm tone, more befitting a grandpa telling a bedtime story than a special agent recalling serial murders.

Once upon a time, some twenty years ago, seven women were killed. All died of asphyxiation, either from hanging or by manual strangulation. Their bodies were displayed with wrists in handcuffs, a square of duct tape over the mouth and a bandanna blindfold. All were in or near a lighthouse. The killer sent notes and audio tapes, taunting law enforcement.

She asked, "Have you stayed in touch with other investigators from the case?"

"Occasionally I check in with the former police chief, Jimi Kim, who retired several years ago. He's a third generation native of Astoria. The current chief, Vivienne, is his granddaughter."

"Deep roots."

"Astoria was founded in 1811 and was one of the oldest permanent settlements west of the Rockies. Early residents were mostly sailors and trappers. Now, the coast guard has a base there."

While he filled in details, she noticed the afternoon skies fading from clear to misty gray and then darker as the haze obscured the sunlight. "Fog."

"Get used to it, newbie."

"I know plenty about fog. I grew up in San Francisco."

"Astoria is one of the foggiest towns in North America. That's why there are so many lighthouses in this area."

"Hence the Lightkeeper moniker," she said. "Do you believe the current murder is connected to what happened twenty years ago?"

"Gotta be. Too similar to be a coincidence."

"The work of a copycat."

"That's a possibility, but don't be too quick to make assumptions."

"I understand." She realized that he'd given her the lesson for the day. Her instincts might be useful but were only one piece of an investigation. They needed research, witnesses and evidentiary facts.

The short bridge over the John Day River gave Skylar a shiver, and she closed her eyes for a moment, waiting for her vertigo to dissipate.

"Tired?" Crawford asked.

"A little bit." She'd never told him or anybody else in the FBI about her phobia. Special agents weren't supposed to have psychological issues.

"I've got a warning for you. The people in Astoria, including local law enforcement, don't always follow the rules. We need to be open."

"Got it."

"Flexible."

"I'm as bendy as a yoga guru."

When they entered Astoria, she peered through fog at a port town of steep hillsides, docks, kitschy businesses and an array of Victorian and Edwardian renovations. She stared at the dominant structure.

Massive. Terrifying. The landmark Astoria-Megler Bridge

spanned the mighty Columbia River between Oregon and Washington.

Her breath caught in her throat. "Yikes."

"The longest cantilevered truss bridge in the country, it's more than twice as long as the Golden Gate. Cape Disappointment is on the opposite side." Crawford pulled into a space outside a rectangular, no-frills structure on 30th Street, a few blocks up from the riverfront. He turned toward her and asked, "Did you ever see the movie *The Goonies*?"

"A long time ago."

"Filmed in Astoria. The opening scene took place at the real-life Clatsop County Jail. Years ago, that old-time prison was transformed into a film museum. This less colorful Public Safety Building is home for the APD, the Astoria Police Department."

They left the Suburban in the parking area and walked around a news van, which was *not*—in Skylar's opinion—a welcome sight. Though she'd only been in Portland for a couple of weeks, she'd already had a confrontation with a cranky on-the-scene reporter who thought she was "too big for her britches."

At the corner of the building was a three-foot-tall iron fence surrounding a pink plaster pig with black hoofs. *More local color?* She pointed. "What's this?"

"The pig started as a prank thirty years ago. Now he's a mascot."

Turning her back on the bridge, she went up the sidewalk toward the entrance. The door to the building opened, and a man strode toward them. The first thing she noticed about him was his height, probably six feet six inches—a full twelve inches taller than she was. His clothing—khakis, a dark blue fleece vest and a plaid shirt with sleeves rolled up—was casual but impeccably neat, which caused her to suspect he was former military. When his laser-blue gaze found her, she felt a burst of electricity and a sizzle she hadn't experienced in quite some time.

Large and in charge, he exuded confidence. He reached out and grasped her hand. "I'm Detective Jake Armstrong."

"Pleased to meet you, Detective." She studied his features. The stubborn set of his square jaw. The dimple centered on his chin. His sharp cheekbones and those amazing blue eyes.

"It's Jake," he said. "I heard the FBI had been summoned. I guess that's you two."

"I'm Skylar," she said. "Special Agent Skylar Gambel."

She felt his gaze sizing her up. Tilting her head back, she did the same to him, continuing her observation and trying to withhold judgment. She guessed his age to be close to thirty. He fit neatly into his environment, and she easily imagined him as a seaman at the helm or a lumberjack. Certainly not an urban transplant like her.

He pushed his dark blond hair off his forehead and zeroed in on her partner. "If I'm not mistaken, you're Special Agent Harold Crawford. You were with the task force that investigated the Lightkeeper twenty years ago."

"Correct."

"We need to talk."

What about me? Skylar wanted to talk with Jake for several reasons. Number one, she wanted information on the prior investigations. Number two, she didn't want to be left out of the loop. And number three...she couldn't explain but wanted to make sense of this attraction to a small-town officer she probably had nothing in common with.

SSA Crawford cleared his throat. "Is Chief Vivienne in the office?"

"Yes, sir. I'm on my way to the crime scene at Cape Meares."

"Perfect." Skylar stepped forward. "I'll ride with you."

Crawford—her supervisor and mentor—gave her a long,

thoughtful look. He often encouraged her to make her own decisions and chart her own course. *Somebody* needed to check out the crime scene. Might as well be her. He raised an eyebrow. "Taking the initiative, newbie?"

"I am, sir."

"First, we meet the chief. Then, you and Detective Armstrong head south to Cape Meares." He turned to Jake. "I remember you from twenty years ago. You loved comic books and were about half the size you are now."

"I was ten."

"You've lived here most of your life," Crawford said. "Were you close to Phoebe Conway?"

His brilliant blue eyes dimmed. "I knew her."

"My condolences," Crawford said. "Astoria has my deepest sympathy. I hope we've arrived in time to prevent other tragic murders."

Chapter Three

Though he would have preferred going to the crime scene and starting his investigation into Phoebe Conway's murder, Jake escorted the two FBI agents into the central lobby of the public safety building where the police and the fire department had their offices. Reporters, bloggers and influencers from Astoria, nearby towns and even Portland—including a threesome of pesky little blondes—had taken up residence, hoping for fresh information on the Lightkeeper's Curse.

Without acknowledging any of them, Jake marched toward the entrance for the APD. Following his lead, neither of the special agents paid attention to the shouted questions. Skylar Gambel—who was prettier than any fed had a right to be—shot angry glares at the local press. Her hostility made him think she'd had negative experiences with reporters.

With her low ponytail at her nape and light makeup, she looked too young to be a world-weary fed, and SSA Crawford had referred to her inexperience. *Newbie?* He'd called her newbie.

Jake didn't get it. Even if Skylar had started just yesterday, he wouldn't have picked that nickname. She owned the sort of cool, sophisticated attitude that went along with being the smartest kid in the room.

He didn't recognize any reporters from the *Astoria Sun*, which was where he'd go after the visit to the crime scene. A short while ago, after Phoebe's identity had been confirmed with fingerprints, Jake had called the newspaper where she worked, talked to the editor and told him that Phoebe's desk should be treated as a crime scene. Nobody should touch anything. Not the other reporters. Or the office staff. Or the janitors. Or Phoebe's friends and family.

He doubted his warning would have much effect, and he sent their primary forensic investigator to enforce his instructions. Asking a flock of newsies to stay away from a potential piece of evidence was akin to advising buzzards that road-kill was off-limits. An unfortunate comparison but accurate.

He hustled Crawford and Skylar into the Astoria Police Department, past the front counter, emblazoned with the Astoria Column logo, and down a hall to the central conference room. The large, windowless space had a long table in the middle, several chairs, a podium pushed to the side, white-boards on easels and the beginnings of a murder board on the wall.

Police Chief Vivienne Kim rose to greet them. "Thanks for your quick response. I hope to take the position of command central for this investigation because my ability to do fieldwork is limited. My doctor advised me to slow down."

Jake pulled a frown to keep from grinning. When the very-pregnant chief turned sideways, the reason for her doctor's advice was evident. A basketball-size bulge puffed out the belly of her dark-blue police uniform jacket. Her badge dangled from a lanyard around her neck. Jake had no idea where she stashed her gun and handcuffs.

She continued, "I suppose I could hand over my responsibilities to somebody else at the APD, but this is the Light-keeper—the worst, most feared serial killer in our town's history. I need to be involved."

"You're handling the situation well," Crawford said. "Your grandpa would be proud."

She flashed a smile and smoothed her straight, shiny black hair. "Jimi always speaks highly of you."

"Not catching the Lightkeeper was one of the great disappointments of both our lives. I hope he can take part in our investigation, even though he's retired."

"So glad you said that. He's on his way in."

Jake watched Skylar's sea-green eyes for a reaction to the irregular protocol of involving a retired officer in police procedure.

Instead of making a comment, she pointed to an open box of Girl Scout cookies. "Are these for everybody?"

"Help yourself," Chief Vivienne said. "We already ate the fruit and quiche, but there's coffee on the side table and hot water for tea. Mugs are in the break room."

"Much appreciated."

Her attitude remained guarded. She seemed to be taking the measure of the APD, forming opinions about the people she'd be working with before deciding how to proceed. Soon she'd discover that Astoria was a small town with a population of about eleven thousand. They had their own ways of doing business.

Chief Kim introduced two other officers in uniform and a local librarian, Dagmar Burke. The chief explained, "I've asked Dagmar to give us context and reminders of the serial killings. She's an expert on local history and the Lightkeeper's Curse."

In Jake's opinion, Dagmar was also headstrong, smug and irritating as all hell. The tall, broad-shouldered woman with tousled blond hair and a boho fashion sense looked down her nose at them and flipped her wrist, setting dozens of sparkly bangles to clanking. "Before I start, do you have any questions?"

"I do," Skylar said. "How many lighthouses are in this area?"

"A lot. Lighthouses were necessary along this stretch of coast that was called the graveyard of the Pacific because of the many shipwrecks. There are dozens of replica lighthouses outside restaurants and shops. A mobile one on a coast guard vessel. Cape Meares, of course, and another on an offshore island near Tillamook. Plus, two more on the Washington side of the Columbia on Cape Disappointment."

"How did Cape Disappointment get its name?" Skylar asked.

"The accepted legend focuses on the British trader, John Meares."

"Who gave his name to the cape farther down the coast."

"That's right." Dagmar launched into lecture mode. "In 1788, while returning from Canada, Meares rounded the cape and ventured into the mouth of the Columbia which was so wide and wild that he thought it was a bay and not the legendary river. The knucklehead went back out to sea. Disappointed. He named the bay, too. Deception Bay."

Jake had spent a lifetime watching Dagmar do her thing and appreciated her encyclopedic grasp of local knowledge. Still, he worried about having her involved in a police investigation, especially this one. She was too close.

"I noticed decorations when we drove through town," Crawford said.

"It's only ten days until Halloween," Dagmar said, "and that's a busy season around here."

"Why?" Skylar asked.

"Fog makes everything look spooky. Astoria developed a rep for having ghosts, hidden pirate treasure and mermaids." In her flowing layers of paisley and fringe, she looked like she'd already costumed herself. "But the most important thing, the only important thing, is solving Phoebe's murder."

"So true," Chief Vivienne said.

Dagmar's cheeks flushed. "I knew Phoebe Conway. She

was a terrific reporter with a big career ahead of her. Had dreams of someday working at one of the Portland television stations. Her murder is tragic."

Though Jake agreed with what she was saying, he worried about the way Dagmar took her friend's death so personally. The last thing they needed was Dagmar getting too wrapped up in her emotions about the case.

Dagmar tossed an accusing comment at SSA Crawford. "This time, you'd better catch the killer."

"Nice to see you again, Dagmar." Crawford kept his tone easygoing. "It was twenty years ago."

"I've changed, and so have you."

"You grew up, and I grew..." Through the grapevine, Jake heard that Crawford was close to the mandatory retirement age of fifty-seven for a special agent. "I grew old."

Skylar stepped up beside her partner but spoke to Dagmar. "I have another question, if you don't mind."

"Shoot," Dagmar said.

"Unlike most of you, I'm new to this case," Skylar said. "I'd like a brief overview of the Lightkeeper's Curse serial murders from the perspective of the locals."

"Go for it, Dagmar." Jake gave her a nod. "Stick to the facts."

"I always do."

"Or not."

"Here's what we know," Dagmar said. "The women were likely stalked. After they were grabbed by the killer, they were held captive for at least two hours but no longer than a day. They were restrained but not tortured. It's unclear what he was doing with them. Or to them."

"I have analysis and victimology reports from twenty years ago," the chief said. "Their ages ranged from nineteen to thirty-nine, and they were diverse in appearance. We'll know more about Phoebe's death after the autopsy."

Dagmar continued, "The Lightkeeper thought he received instructions from an exalted priestess who despised these women for their wanton ways. It was his job to rid the world of them. With each victim, he made a cassette recording of her last moments, giving her a chance to recant her errors. He didn't blindfold and gag them until after they were dead. The Lightkeeper also sent taunting letters to the *Astoria Sun*."

When Skylar glanced at him, looking for answers, he didn't respond. She turned toward the chief and asked, "Was there a note before the murder of Phoebe Conway?"

"We haven't found anything," Chief Kim said.

"Have you received a recording?"

"Not yet."

"What about the curse?" Skylar asked.

"I'm an expert on this particular subject." Dagmar's voice quavered. "The last woman he killed, number seven, was my mother. Working as a librarian, she studied curses and killers. Once, she told me and my dad that she thought she was being followed. He didn't believe her, but I did. I was only twelve. There wasn't much I could do."

Skylar spoke in a gentle tone. "I'm so sorry, Dagmar."

She shook her head, and her wild hair danced. "Before she died, my mother cursed him, and he recorded her words. Unlike all the other tapes, he spoke on this one and whispered that he was sorry. Mama was his last victim."

Until now?

Chapter Four

After leaving the APD, Skylar walked beside Jake to the parking area where he headed toward a dark gray Ford Explorer with the Astoria police logo on the side. The midafternoon fog was even thicker than when she and Crawford had arrived in town less than an hour ago. She stood at the passenger side of Jake's car and inhaled a gulp of salty harbor air while he unlocked the door and opened it for her.

Seated inside, she tried to center herself as she considered Dagmar's lecture about the twenty-year-old serial murders. The Lightkeeper typified the worst kind of serial killer—an intelligent individual with an organized plan for his assaults, ranging from stalking to staging the bodies while sending written and verbal taunts to the police. Investigating him would be a challenge, for sure. And potentially a failure. He'd escaped before.

Not that they had proof the person who killed Phoebe was the infamous Lightkeeper. The similarity between twenty years ago and the current murder could be coincidence. Or the work of a copycat.

The description of a killer who was on a "mission" and had guidance from a mysterious priestess made her think of the Son of Sam, a serial killer in New York in the seventies who claimed to be taking orders from his neighbor's dog. Hearing voices was symptomatic of several forms of psychosis. Skylar would leave it to the profilers to analyze, but she needed to understand the Lightkeeper's motives.

Thus far, no one had mentioned sexual molestation. Why did the Lightkeeper kill? And why did he quit? She found it hard to believe this brutal murderer was stopped by a curse.

She asked Jake, "How well do you know Dagmar?"

"Why do you ask?"

He didn't answer her question, and she noticed the deflection. His indirect response gave rise to suspicions about him. Not for the first time, she sensed a cover-up in his attitude. Something to do with Dagmar? Their back-and-forth banter had a familiar, teasing edge. She wouldn't have been surprised to discover that they were or had been close, possibly ex-girlfriend and boyfriend. Or something more. He wasn't wearing a wedding ring. "Did you and Dagmar both grow up in Astoria?"

"Yes, but I got out as soon as I turned eighteen."

"Joined the military?" she guessed.

"Marines."

Skylar scored a point for her instincts and returned to the topic at hand. "I'm surprised Dagmar didn't move away. Having her mother murdered by a serial killer must have triggered post-traumatic stress disorder. Tell me again what she does for a living. A historian?"

"Librarian," he said.

"Like her mother," she said. "She's a great storyteller. Not revealing the words to the curse was a master touch. I'm curious. Do you know what it said?"

"Yes."

Of course, he did. "Because the police have the cassette recording of Dagmar's mother's last words. You've gone back and listened to it."

"I heard the tape when the murders took place."

"But you were only a kid, right?"

He turned right onto a street that followed the harbor, and they passed the historic red-and-yellow trolley that dinged a bell, enticing Halloween tourists to ride. "I shouldn't have heard the recording when I was so young, but the former police chief encouraged my interest."

"Chief Jimi Kim." Crawford had praised this retired officer to the skies. "Surely, he didn't share evidence with you."

"He was too good a cop to break evidentiary protocol or procedure. But I was determined, and I got my sticky little fingers on a copy of the tape."

"You stole it."

"Borrowed," he said. "The audio quality wasn't great. You can hear every word, but voice analysis of the Lightkeeper's whisper was inconclusive when he said he was sorry. Couldn't even tell if it was a man or a woman."

She was about to ask him to repeat the curse when she noticed their route past a marina where fishing boats were docked. "Where are we headed?"

"South. We take Highway 101 all the way to Cape Meares after we cross the bridge."

The bridge? Panic shot through her. "I thought the bridge went to Washington."

"You're thinking of the Astoria-Megler Bridge—the colossus that looms over Astoria like Godzilla. This is the New Youngs Bay Bridge. In comparison, it's a baby bridge. A two-lane drive, not very high and shorter than a mile."

Peering through the fog, she saw the Explorer approaching the bay as if to dive nose first through the fog and into the water. No time to prepare herself. She couldn't settle her breathing. Or meditate. Or shield herself in any way from her irrational phobia. Not even her mantra—*Nam myoho renge kyo*—could help. Probably she had those syllables twisted and wrong. *Can't do anything right.* Her tension escalated. Her pulse fluttered like a caged bird.

When he drove onto the bridge, she slammed her eyes closed. Less than a mile. She could hold her breath for that long. In her head, she started playing a song with a heavy beat. "Proud Mary" usually distracted her. Again, she couldn't remember the words. "…left a good job in the city…" The rumble of tires on concrete competed with her song. "…rolling, rolling, rolling on the river."

"Skylar?"

She heard concern in his voice and hoped that she hadn't been singing out loud. Her eyelids lifted. *Hallelujah*, the Explorer was on solid ground.

Jake asked, "Are you okay? You look pale."

"A little hungry, that's all." She forced a smile. "What were we talking about?"

"Come to think of it," he said, "I skipped lunch, too. We can make a stop. Grab a burger."

"I'd rather get to the crime scene." She dug into her purse and pulled out a granola bar. "I'll munch on this. Weren't you going to tell me more about the curse?"

He didn't look convinced that an energy bar would put everything right. "I'm stopping at the next drive-through for coffee and a muffin."

"Suit yourself." She managed to inhale a deep, oxygen-rich breath and hoped she'd recovered. "You were going to reveal the magic words of the curse."

"Not magic," he said. "And Dagmar's mom wasn't a witch."

"Okay." This point seemed important to him, and she wondered why.

"Here's what you need to keep in mind. All the victims were blindfolded and gagged with hands cuffed behind their back. All were strangled."

She bit a chunk from the energy bar, chewed slowly and swallowed. "Did Dagmar's mother know about the blindfolds and such?"

"Everybody knew. This is a small town."

"Got it."

He stared through the windshield, looking every bit like a solid, sane, steady detective. A marine. Jake didn't seem like the sort of man who would worry about curses and witches. He recited from memory:

"Hear me, o goddesses,
West, East, North, South.
Scratch out his eyes.
Muzzle his mouth.

Rip off his ears.
Silence his plea.
Death to the Keeper.
So mote it be."

An involuntary shiver rippled down Skylar's spine. Not magic but definitely morbid and creepy. "How did Dagmar's mother come up with this curse?"

"She put it together from various fictions and legends. When she says it on the tape, her words are trembling. Not with fear but with rage. She demands revenge."

And her fierce energy was enough to intimidate the killer. Skylar wanted to believe in the power and strength of Dagmar's mother, but she couldn't help thinking of other possibilities. The Lightkeeper packed up and moved away from Astoria. Or was incarcerated for another crime. Or died.

She turned her head and gazed at a view of the Pacific beyond the sandy beach and roadside shops. The Astoria fog had begun to lift as soon as they left the harbor. Sunlight sparkled on the waves. The offshore rock formations created dramatic vistas. "What do you call those rocks?"

"Sea stacks," he said. "Formed by wave and wind erosion. Many are basalt, volcanic in origin. Some of them are hundreds of feet high—like Haystack Rock, which isn't far from where we're headed. They have their own environments with nesting seabirds and other mammals."

The stacks made her think of guardians protecting the coast and keeping the ships away. "I'm guessing those rocks are part of the reason for the many lighthouses."

"It's a hell of a rugged coast." Though Jake usually didn't waste time and effort on humor, he added, "Living in Oregon ain't for sissies."

Especially when they hate bridges.

When he exited from the highway and drove to the carry-out window for a coffee shop, she was grateful for the caffeine and the blueberry muffins. Another factoid she'd learned about her new home state: they made great coffee in the Pacific Northwest.

She snuggled into her seat and watched the fog drift away. The skies weren't totally blue. But not murky gray, either. She felt more optimistic about her first assignment in the field. The drive to the Cape Meares crime scene would take about an hour and a half, which ought to be enough time to recover her equilibrium and focus her attention on the crime scene.

Chapter Five

Jake parked at the scenic overlook off Highway 101 where signage identified important sights and their historical significance as well as pointed the way to the famous Octopus Tree, a Sitka spruce with eight trunks, and the pathway leading to Cape Meares Lighthouse.

The parking spaces were filled with vehicles: another Explorer from the APD, sedans from the Clackamas County sheriff's office and from the Oregon State Police, a few more SUVs from the Oregon Park Service and the Tillamook County sheriff's office, plus three unmarked cars and a van that belonged to the department of the Warrenton medical examiner. Jurisdiction would be a bitch unless Special Agent Skylar Gambel took control right from the start.

She hadn't been chatty on the drive down here, except for a few phone calls, and Jake appreciated the silence. They both had a lot to think about, starting with finding the person who killed Phoebe Conway and making sure the murderer didn't strike again.

Skylar's attack of nervousness on the drive from Astoria worried him, but she had herself completely under control as she exited the Explorer. The lady knew what she was doing. She wore her gray suit and her FBI windbreaker like armor. Allowing himself to appreciate her athletic stride and the confident set of her shoulders, he watched her stalk toward the Tillamook deputy sheriff with his six-pointed star badge visible on his light brown uniform. He stood like a sentinel at the top of an asphalt path, wide enough for a vehicle, that led into the forest.

Skylar displayed her FBI credentials as she introduced herself to the deputy sheriff and a couple of other officers who had gathered.

The deputy scowled, acting tough. "I arrived immediately after the park ranger called. I secured the area, contacted the relevant people and instructed the ME to remove the body."

She glared at the streamers of yellow-and-black crime scene tape draped around the viewing area and pathways like prom decorations. "We received a preliminary packet of info and photos. I didn't see a forensics report on the cars you found here or on tire tracks."

"Nothing to report." The deputy deepened his scowl and puffed out his chest. Arrogant. Antagonistic. Stupid.

"You found no evidence whatsoever," Skylar said in a disbelieving tone.

"It rained last night. Any kind of dusty footprints would be washed away. That blue Subaru Legacy was parked here when we arrived. It belongs to the victim."

"Which you know," she said, "because you forced the locks."

"Didn't have to. The car keys were in her purse."

"Which you removed from the murder scene."

"Yeah, we did," he said defensively. "We needed her ID."

"Did your forensic investigators process the car?"

"I didn't think it was necessary."

"You were wrong," Skylar said. "Attention to detail is how cases get solved. As of now, the FBI has control of this jurisdiction. You may return to your vehicle and stay out of the way unless I need you, which seems unlikely."

"You can't waltz in here and take over."

"I just did." She didn't scoff but her disgust was apparent as she scanned the four other officers who hovered around. "All of you, step aside until I have further instructions."

When she charged down the asphalt path, the deputy jumped out of her way so quickly that he almost tripped. She didn't spare him a glance. Her focus was directed toward the lighthouse.

Jake walked beside her. He wasn't about to complain about her abrupt attitude with the Tillamook deputy whose sloppy handling of the scene deserved reprimand. He hoped the APD officers who reported to him and were waiting at the lighthouse had done a better job.

A rough wood railing on the downward sloping path held back forest on one side. The other side was at the edge of a high cliff with only occasional trees and shrubs. A spectacular, panoramic view stretched all the way to the horizon. Closer to shore, the surf crashed against sea stacks, sending up plumes of white surf.

Skylar glanced at him and said, "When I talked to Crawford on the phone, he said he'd already given the okay for the FBI forensic team from Portland to document and analyze the crime scene. He also mentioned that Dr. Kate Kinski, the Warrenton ME, had good people working for her who could help."

"I have two officers here," he said. "They've both undergone training sessions and know how to do the basics, like fingerprints and the photos they already sent to APD headquarters. We welcome the opportunity to assist the experts."

"This is an unusual case." They rounded a curve on the path and came into sight of the top of the lighthouse on the rocky promontory below them. "Even without the historic connection to the Lightkeeper, the circumstances are odd."

"You've got that right."

When she met his gaze, he noticed a sparkle in her sea-green eyes. Her full lips quirked in a grin. Not of amusement but satisfaction. He could tell she was looking forward to checking out the scene. Almost like a kid on Christmas Eve. Somewhat ghoulish, but he understood—Jake felt the same way.

The Cape Meares Lighthouse stood only thirty-eight feet tall. The pathway wrapped around the base provided another stunning view at the seaward edge. Skylar asked, "Why is this tower so stubby?"

"It's built on a two-hundred-foot-tall cliff, which makes it visible far out to sea."

They approached the two APD officers—Dub Wagner and Dot Holman—who stood outside the door to the gift shop. Both officers nodded to Skylar and shook her hand when Jake introduced them.

"Who took the crime scene photos?" Skylar asked.

"I did," Dot said. "They were okay, weren't they?"

"Better than okay. The pictures gave an accurate idea of scale and showed several angles. I'm glad you recorded the position of Phoebe's purse before that deputy messed with the scene. Good work, Dot."

"Thank you, ma'am." She was probably the same age as Skylar but gave her a *ma'am* out of respect. A small woman, Dot looked like she was wearing a child-size uniform costume. "I work part-time for the ME, so dead bodies don't bother me."

Not to be outdone, Dub—short for *W* because his first name was Wallace and the last was Wagner, making him a *W* double—spoke up. "First thing we noticed when we got here was the light. Since this lighthouse has been decommissioned, the beacon isn't lit."

Jake encouraged him to say more. "What else?"

"The light over the door doesn't work. There's still a bulb, but we didn't touch it."

"Because there might be fingerprints," Dot added.

"On the inside of the gift shop," Dub said, "none of the overhead lights were turned on, which makes sense now because it's daylight. But we think it was dark in the shop last night."

"What led to that conclusion?" Jake asked, playing along with the gradual reveal of clues.

Dub and Dot led them to the door of the gift shop. Before they entered, Dub produced a box containing Tyvek booties and protective gloves. Jake covered his shoes, proud that his team had paid attention in the forensic classes.

Inside the gift shop, Dub pointed toward the cash register behind the counter where five lighthouse replicas, each three feet tall, lined up in a row.

Dot scampered toward them and activated the battery-operated lights. They all flashed alternating red and white. "These were working when we arrived this morning," she said, "and I'll bet they were on last night."

Jake imagined what it must have been like for Phoebe when she stepped from the darkness outdoors into the shop and was confronted with these touristy strobe lights. Disconcerted. Confused. Phoebe wouldn't have come here by chance. "What was the time of death?"

Dot answered, "According to Dr. Kinski, preliminary estimate of TOD is between midnight and 2:00 a.m."

To Skylar, Jake said, "Phoebe's car is in the lot. She must have driven herself. This late-night rendezvous was prearranged."

"Unless she drove with the killer."

"If she drove, how would he get home?"

"He or she," Skylar said. She was correct. They hadn't determined gender.

"Phoebe must have been concerned about the person she was supposed to meet. She brought a weapon." He pointed to the stun gun on the floor and said to Dot, "You sent photos of the gun and her flashlight. Were these objects moved from their original position?"

"The Tillamook deputy had already removed the purse. And we turned off the flashing lights to preserve the batteries. But we didn't let anybody touch anything else," Dot said in the no-nonsense tone she probably used with her three preteen kids. "We wanted to preserve the scene for you and Special Agent Gambel."

If Phoebe had seen her attacker coming, Jake figured that she would have reacted. Fight or flight, she would have taken her shot with the stun gun or tried to run…or frozen in place. The deer-in-the-headlights response was not uncommon.

Skylar strolled through the shelves and racks of merchandise, leaving the gift shop and entering the adjoining lighthouse tower, which was set up with educational display photos and posters. She tapped the wall switch, bathing the circular wrought iron staircase in light. "The body was found in here."

"That's right," Dub said. "We didn't want her to be moved, but Dr. Kinski said she'd take full responsibility."

"You handled the situation properly," Jake assured him. Cooperation with the ME was the right thing to do. The doc recognized the references to the Lightkeeper, notified the FBI and recommended that they be brought into the investigation quickly. Obviously, the right call.

His gaze fixed on the first curve where the killer had arranged Phoebe's body. The photos showed her sitting with her legs tucked under her on the lowest step. One of her sneakers had fallen off her foot, revealing a striped sock. Maybe she'd lost her shoe in a struggle. When he squinted, he could imagine seeing her with wrists cuffed, a bandanna blindfold and duct tape over her mouth.

"What else did you notice about Phoebe?" Skylar asked the APD officers.

"Her hair was combed and smooth," Dub said. "She hadn't

been out in the rain, which means she was inside before the storm started at eleven minutes past midnight."

"What about cuts or bruises?" Skylar asked. "Were there injuries that didn't show in the photos?"

"Her arms and legs were covered by her clothes so we couldn't see much." Dub cringed at the memory. "Her throat was bruised, probably from being choked to death."

"I doubt she was killed in that artistic position on the staircase." Skylar glanced around the room. "Strangulation could have taken place on the floor in here. Or outside on the path before it rained, which is less likely because her clothes aren't dirty. When the forensic team processes this area, ask them to watch for signs of where she was attacked. The location."

"Yes, ma'am," Dub responded.

"After she was killed, she had to be moved to the staircase." Skylar pantomimed picking up the body and carrying it. "Takes physical strength to do that."

"You bet it does," Dub said. "It's hard to transport dead weight."

"Did Dr. Kinski assign a COD?" Skylar asked.

"Cause of death is homicide," Dot said with a shrug. "The Tillamook County coroner agreed. I expect we'll learn more after the autopsy is done."

"Like if she was drugged," Jake said. In addition to the absence of cuts and bruises, her clothes weren't torn, which led him to suspect she'd been sedated before being strangled.

Skylar gave him a nod. "I'll check with my partner to find out if we're going to transport Phoebe to the Portland medical examiner or leave the body with Dr. Kinski."

"The Lightkeeper murders were before her time," Jake said, "but Kinski has access to all the old files, and she can consult with the guy who did the autopsies twenty years ago."

"She's also close enough that we can go to her facility and observe," Skylar said. "But it's not my call."

Her cool professionalism and awareness of protocol impressed him. He had absolutely no reason to be concerned about her handling of the crime scene or the many and varied law enforcement officers who turned up to help. Their good intentions might lead to sloppy evidence. Like Skylar had said, *Attention to detail is how cases get solved.* He liked her by-the-book approach. Unfortunately, he had a personal issue that might jeopardize the investigation.

He waited until they'd finished up at the Cape Meares Lighthouse, left Dot and Dub to wait for the Portland-based FBI forensic team and returned to his Explorer before he mentioned the potential problem. After he exited the parking area at the scenic overlook and merged onto Highway 101 headed north, he said, "When you first arrived, I mentioned that I needed to talk to Special Agent Crawford. It occurs to me that you are the person I need to speak with."

"Go ahead, I'm listening."

"I have a conflict of interest."

Chapter Six

Skylar swiveled around in the passenger seat of the Explorer so she could give Jake her full attention. Their visit to the crime scene had gone well. The Astoria officers, Dot and Dub, had kept the interior of the lighthouse relatively untouched, despite having to turn Phoebe's body over to the medical examiner. Skylar had been particularly impressed when Dot had insisted they wear the Tyvek booties. Jake's observations had been on point and efficient, so much so that she wondered how many complicated cases this backwoods detective had managed. His logic matched her own.

She didn't want to hear about a problem he was having with the investigation, but she had no choice. "Tell me about this so-called conflict of interest."

"First, I want to give you context," he said. "We've got the time. It's a long drive back to Astoria."

And another crossing of the bridge across the bay. "Still listening."

"Twenty years ago, the Lightkeeper murders interested me. I won't say *obsessed* because I, frankly, didn't know what that word meant when I was ten. Anyway, I liked the idea of fitting pieces together and catching a bad guy. Saving innocent lives appealed to me almost as much as the sci-fi heroes in my comic books. In a way, the Lightkeeper's Curse might have convinced me to become a cop."

"Was this before or after you stole a piece of evidence?"

"I returned the tape. Nobody even noticed it was gone."

"Really?" she said skeptically. "Let's not push former Police Chief Jimi Kim for an answer on that topic."

"After I joined the APD, I decided I wasn't cut out to be a cop who did nothing but give traffic citations. I'm a detective, born to investigate." He glanced across the center console toward her. "I suspect you're the same way."

His perceptions hit close to home. She'd gone through several false starts before she was appointed to field duty as a special agent, which was what she really wanted to do. So far, she'd enjoyed the investigation and found satisfaction uncovering evidence. Being a federal officer with jurisdictional control also appealed to her. She and Jake were more alike than she would have guessed. *A City mouse and a country mouse are still both mice.*

She studied his profile as he kept his eyes on the road. Though the fog had somewhat dissipated, and skies were relatively clear, she didn't need her dark glasses. The late afternoon sun highlighted his high cheekbones and sharp jawline. Staring at his face felt a bit disconcerting. Made her remember the sizzle that zapped through her when they first met. Not that she had any intention of forming a personal relationship with this man.

"Six degrees of separation," he said. "Are you familiar with that concept?"

"Of course. The idea is that all people are separated by a chain of six or fewer social connections."

"In a small town like Astoria, when seven women are murdered, it's a spiderweb of connections. So many people are touched."

"Like Dagmar Burke," she said. "It was a shock to find out her mother was a victim."

"Exactly like Dagmar. She's a good example of what can

happen when someone close to the victim gets tangled up in the investigation. In Dagmar's view, her mom was a saint who cursed the Lightkeeper and ended his reign of terror. A lot of people disagreed. Some in town considered her mother to be a witch who whispered secret messages to the Lightkeeper. Others thought Mama Burke was a dangerous crackpot."

She appreciated his insight but recognized his stalling technique. During this drive back to Astoria, cocooned in his Explorer, they could go on forever, tossing theories back and forth. She didn't have the patience. "All right, Armstrong, what exactly is your problem?"

"Victim number seven, Dagmar's mother, was my aunt. After her death, my dad took Dagmar in and raised her as his own. My cousin became the sister I never had."

Skylar swallowed hard. His cousin? That explained their teasing conversation and clearly illustrated why he shouldn't be part of the investigation. A close family relationship was, in fact, a giant conflict of interest. He might be focused on revenge or overwhelmed by survivor's guilt or angry because the killer was never caught. No wonder he hid this relationship from her. "I ought to boot you off this case."

"Do what you need to do," he said. "But I'm not going to quit my investigation. I'll resign from the APD and pursue the investigation on my own. As a private investigator."

"Can you do that?" she asked.

"The state of Oregon requires a license, but I qualify."

Obviously, the investigation was deeply important to him. "You're dedicated," she said.

"That's right."

"Also, annoying."

"Right, again."

When SSA Crawford had told her to expect idiosyncrasies from the Astoria end of the investigation, he hadn't been exaggerating. These people operated in unique, eccentric ways.

If they'd been in Portland, she would have been more likely to take Jake off the case. In Astoria, he had an advantage. He knew everyone in town. His perspective could make a difference. "I hate to lose you as an asset."

"That's pretty much what Chief Vivienne said."

Skylar suspected that SSA Crawford also knew that Jake and Dagmar were part of the same family. And her partner hadn't demanded that Jake step down. Nor would she.

Jake could stay.

"Here's the deal, Armstrong. No more secrets."

"Fair enough." A smile lifted the corner of his mouth. "We'll work together."

"We'll try."

He wasted no time suggesting the direction for their investigation. "Our next stop should be the newspaper where Phoebe Conway worked. The *Astoria Sun*."

"An ironic name for a newspaper in a town that's always foggy."

"We try not to take ourselves too seriously."

During the rest of their drive, they reviewed their observations from the crime scene. Logical conclusions: the killer planned the time and place for the meeting. Phoebe drove herself. She suspected trouble and brought a stun gun for protection. At the gift shop, the killer turned off lights and ambushed Phoebe. Cause of death was strangulation. Her body was posed on the staircase after being blindfolded and having her mouth covered with duct tape.

When they approached the bridge across the bay, Skylar used yogic breathing, closed her eyes and filled her head with her favorite mantra. Apart from the shortness of breath, she did okay. After living in Portland with all the bridges, she'd discovered that after she crossed the same bridge once or twice or more, her phobia lessened. Also, it helped that dusk had begun to settle, and her vision wasn't glaringly clear.

In downtown Astoria, streetlights sliced through the fog and illuminated neon skeleton decorations. Halloween was one of her favorite holidays; it granted people the permission to dress up and become someone else. She happily devoured gobs of chocolate and danced until dawn at wild, macabre parties. Her parents celebrated with elaborate haunted house decorations at their multimillion-dollar home in San Francisco's Nob Hill. Her brothers, both lawyers, usually dressed as bloodsucking vampires, and her mom—a superior court judge—achieved citywide fame with her sexy Morticia Addams costume.

Jake parked the Explorer at the curb down the street from the storefront office of the *Astoria Sun*. His forensic guy claimed to have uncovered important evidence at Phoebe's workplace, and she was eager to learn more.

The office was an open bullpen about the size of a basketball court where several clunky gray desks denoted separate work areas for reporters and salespeople. Overhead, black-and-orange streamers dangled from strings spread like a giant spiderweb on the ceiling. Across the back and down one side, a half wall separated other offices. The upper glass portion of those offices had also been decorated with odd, grotesque drawings.

A skinny, raven-haired young woman dressed all in black perched on a high stool behind the front counter. Halloween had come early for her. She looked like a witch in heavy makeup. Her nameplate read Tabitha Previn. In case the casual observer missed the identification, she wore a necklace with *Tabby* written in silver. At the sight of Detective Armstrong, she clutched a hand with long black fingernails to her breast and nearly swooned.

"Oh my goodness." She bounced to her feet, rushed around the counter and flung herself into his arms. "I can't believe it. Phoebe is dead."

He gently patted her back. "You and Phoebe were close."

"Not besties, but we spent a lot of time together."

"I understand."

"I know you do, Jake. More than anybody, you understand death and murder."

Skylar looked away from the awkward display of one-sided affection and surveyed the office where plastic pumpkins, fanged vampire bats, black cats and witches' cauldrons competed with the yellow crime scene tape draped around a desk to the left of the front counter. Only three other people were in the bullpen, and they gave a wide berth to the designated scene where a guy wearing nitrile gloves tapped keys on a laptop. No doubt, he was the forensic expert assigned by Jake.

The protocol disturbed her. The APD should have waited for the FBI experts to process this scene. Her training as both a lawyer and at Quantico told her they needed to be careful with evidence. Even though she accepted Jake despite his conflict of interest, she wouldn't let the investigation be handled with casual disregard.

Jake introduced her to Alan Quilling, head of APD's forensic department. Like Dot, he also worked as a part-time assistant to the Clatsop County medical examiner in Warrenton. Instead of shaking hands, he flapped his long fingers in a clumsy wave. When he stood, she realized he was another tall guy. Clearly over six feet, he was as long-necked and skinny as the sandhill cranes on the coast. He peeked through circular wire-rimmed glasses. "Special Agent Gambel, you're going to like what I've found. Starting with this. It was locked in her top right drawer." He held up a cell phone.

Instead of taking it, Skylar reached into her purse, found a pair of her own gloves and slipped them on. "Have you checked for fingerprints?"

"First thing," he said. "There are only Phoebe's prints."

Jake stepped up beside her. "Did you figure out the password?"

"Tabitha told me." Quilling cast a shy smile toward the receptionist. "She's very helpful."

Surprised that Phoebe had trusted anyone else with her password, Skylar glanced at Tabitha who had followed them to Phoebe's workspace and stood close to Jake while reapplying her black lipstick. Skylar asked, "Did Phoebe usually leave her phone in her desk?"

"Sometimes but not often," Tabitha said. "That's her work phone, which is why I have the password. She took her personal phone everywhere."

Jake reminded Skylar, "The personal phone was in Phoebe's car at Cape Meares."

And would be a useful source of leads from people she'd spoken to recently. Contacting the carrier for a listing of her recent calls was standard procedure. "Did you follow up?"

"Chief Kim is taking care of it. Not sure if she has the data yet."

Skylar turned back to Tabitha. "Can you think of a reason she might have left this phone at work?"

"I know why," Quilling said cheerfully. He punched a few buttons on the phone and brought up a photo of an envelope with Phoebe's name and the address of the *Astoria Sun*. The next photo showed a note that had been printed off a computer.

"She was instructed not to bring her phone."

Skylar leaned closer and squinted.

Helpfully, Quilling said, "I can read it for you."

"Please don't." Outraged and appalled to be discussing sensitive evidence in the middle of the *Astoria Sun* newspaper bullpen, she turned to Jake and raised her eyebrows, silently asking why he wasn't taking charge. Quilling shouldn't be waving Phoebe's phone around for everybody to see.

She snapped at Quilling, "Put the phone in an evidence bag and give it to me."

"Okay." He bobbed his head, and his mop of brown hair fell across his forehead.

"Stop your investigation immediately but leave the crime scene tape in place. Stay right here and wait for the Portland FBI forensic team to arrive."

"Yes, ma'am."

She snatched the clear plastic bag with the phone and steamed toward the exit, barely able to control her frustration and anger. The sloppy handling of evidence merited a serious talking-to, at the very least. On the sidewalk outside the *Sun*, she pivoted and hiked up the incline toward the curb where the Explorer was parked. Jake should have trained Quilling more effectively, should have explained the chain of custody as pertained to evidence.

She came to a halt, belatedly aware that she'd also broken the rules by grabbing the phone and stalking out the door. Losing control. Making mistakes. She needed to settle down before she blew her first assignment as a field agent.

Jake jogged up beside her. "Hang on a minute."

Rather than engaging in an embarrassing chase down the street, she faced him. "Detective, I'm shocked and dismayed by the APD's handling of this case, starting with Chief Kim allowing Dagmar, a civilian, to take part as an expert."

He nodded.

"Involving her grandpa, even if he is a retired police chief, isn't correct procedure." She suspected SSA Crawford would disagree and welcome Jimi into the investigation, but that didn't mean she had to approve. "And then, there's Quilling. There are important procedural reasons for following the rules of evidence. Quilling behaved badly. As his supervisor, you should have stopped him."

He stood silently, waiting for her to continue, but she'd run out of complaints.

She held up the plastic evidence bag—an unspoken admission that she, too, made mistakes. "We need to log this in to evidence."

"First, let's take a closer look at that note on Phoebe's work phone."

"Not here. Not while we're standing on the sidewalk. Didn't I just ream Quilling for being too casual with evidence?"

He gestured toward the Explorer parked at the curb. "Is that private enough?"

"We've been in the car all day." She glanced over her shoulder at a coffee shop on the corner. "And I'm starving."

They ducked inside the shop where Jake knew the woman behind the counter. *Of course, he does.* After placing a quick order for lattes, premade sandwiches and potato chips, they went to a circular table in the corner away from the windows to wait for their coffee. Carefully, she cleared a space, removed the phone from the see-through evidence bag and held it so he could read the message on the screen:

I have new evidence about the Lightkeeper's Curse Murders. You should be the reporter to tell this story, Phoebe. You're a shining star from the Lone Star state but unappreciated. I'll make sure you get what you deserve. Tell no one about this contact. Don't bring a phone or a camera. Cape Meares Lighthouse at midnight.

"It's clever," she said, "the way he praises her abilities as a reporter and promises a scoop on the Lightkeeper."

"Phoebe was ambitious. Doesn't surprise me that she decided to take the risk and follow his rules. The person who sent this note knew her weakness."

She realized that the note was more important than her frustration, Quilling's incompetence and her own imprecise handling of the evidence. "There's more to be found at the newspaper. I'm afraid we're not done there."

"Not by a long shot."

She turned off the phone and returned it to the evidence bag. "First, we try to find out how the note was delivered. Then we check with the editor about possible follow-up messages from the killer. That's how the Lightkeeper operated twenty years ago, right?"

"He left notes or sent letters," Jake said.

"Technology has improved. The present-day Lightkeeper will probably use the contact email for the *Sun*."

"No doubt."

They were back on the same page. Working together to solve Phoebe's murder.

Chapter Seven

Across the tiny, round table, Jake's gaze met hers. In her eyes, he saw an unwavering intelligence that compelled him to look more closely, past the sea green tint and the flecks of gold into their depths. She reached behind her head and unfastened the ponytail at her nape. Thick auburn waves tumbled to her shoulders when she tossed her head.

Pretty but tough as nails, she seemed to like being in charge. The FBI outranked local police, and Skylar was a natural boss lady. When she'd snarled at mild-mannered Quilling, Jake had seen her slender fingers clench into fists. He halfway expected her to bop Quilling on top of his pointy head. Maybe he shouldn't have found her kickass attitude attractive, but he did.

To hide his grin, Jake dropped his gaze and focused on her feet under the table. The ankle boots peeking out from her trousers were stylish and probably had steel toes for kicking butt. She was that type of woman.

She twisted the top off her chocolate chip muffin and took a large bite. Not a dainty eater. Another plus in her favor. She gave a happy moan. "Yummmm."

Though he could have spent hours observing her and imagining what made her tick, there was work to be done. He picked up on what she'd said a moment ago about the Lightkeeper sending notes and recordings to the police. Would the same strategy apply to the person who strangled Phoebe? "Technically, the Cape Meares murder can't be considered a serial killing. It was only one death."

"That's why our case is so interesting. It's not often that investigators have access to the initial crime. Plus, there are parallels with the Lightkeeper."

Things were going to get confusing if they continued to call the long-ago serial killer and the person who killed Phoebe by the same name. He asked, "Do you think it's the same guy?"

"Could be a copycat."

"Or a coincidence."

Her full lips twisted into a frown. "Crawford warned me about making assumptions."

"He's right." A good detective kept an open mind.

The woman who had been at the counter brought a tray to their table and added their to-go coffee cups to the sandwiches. Skylar gave her a thumbs-up and took another bite.

He unwrapped his ham and cheese on rye and bit into the center. More than the taste, he appreciated the caloric fuel to energize his lagging brain power. He hadn't eaten since the drive-through on their way to Cape Meares.

Skylar dabbed her lips with a napkin. "If the Lightkeeper from twenty years ago was a young man—in his twenties— he'd only be in his forties now. I could see him coming out of retirement to kill Phoebe Conway. But if he was forty or fifty when he started…"

"He'd be sixty or older now," Jake said.

"Twenty years ago, there must have been a profile. Was he local? Who were the suspects?" She snapped her fingers. "I know who has that information."

"Crawford."

"I'll check with him. Tell him what we're doing. And ask for his on-the-scene analysis from twenty years ago."

"Until then, we need to figure out a way to refer to Phoebe's killer," he said. "To differentiate him from the Lightkeeper in the past."

"Don't worry. He'll give us a name."

"You think he'll tell us what to call him." He sipped his double-shot latte. The caffeine should get him into gear. "How do you figure?"

"That's an educated guess," she said. "Not an assumption."

He didn't see the difference. "Explain."

"From the smug tone evident in his note and the headline-grabbing nature of the murder, I'm guessing he's a big-time narcissist. He'll gobble up all the credit."

Her reasoning seemed sound. "Seems like you do *not* think this is the Lightkeeper from twenty years ago."

"Not sure. But I tend to make accurate guesses. Call it instinct."

They lit into the food and finished eating in mere minutes. Skylar continued to make those moaning sounds. She licked her fingers when she was done. Sophisticated but not prissy. And sexy as hell.

He was glad to have her on his side.

ON THE SIDEWALK outside the coffee shop, the twilight fog draped over Astoria like a tattered shroud. Through the swirls, Skylar caught terrifying glimpses of the massive bridge over the Columbia River. Downhill below the riverwalk, the deep-water port seemed relatively calm. Well-lit vessels docked at the coast guard base waiting patiently for an emergency summons.

Balancing her to-go latte, she hit the speed dial for Crawford's number on her phone. It rang several times before he answered.

Talking fast, his voice sounded hyper when he told her that his files from the twenty-year-old case had taken up much of the conference room at the APD. Jimi had joined him, and they were putting together details from the past. "We had four viable suspects. Two are still in Oregon. I want to interview these guys as soon as possible. When will you be back here?"

"Soon as possible," she said. "We're going to need more assistance from the FBI forensic resources in Portland."

"Such as?"

She ran through their needs at the crime scene, potential surveillance on lighthouses and cybercrimes to be coordinated with Quilling.

He cleared his throat. "And what will you be doing?"

"Jake and I need to follow up at the *Astoria Sun*," she said. "Speaking of Detective Armstrong, you must have known about his family relationship to Dagmar's mother."

"I knew."

But Crawford hadn't mentioned Jake's inappropriate connection to the victim. She wondered if her mentor had been testing her judgment. She sipped her latte. "I'm still wrapping my head around the fact that he's related to one of the murdered women, but I don't have a problem working with him. His knowledge of the town can help."

"Did he know Phoebe Conway?"

She recalled the hugs and snugs he got from Tabitha. He was a good-looking man. An eligible bachelor. "I have a feeling he knows most of the single women in town."

"I have an idea," Crawford said. "We have a lot of ground to cover in this investigation. How about if you and Jake concentrate on Phoebe's murder by talking to her coworkers at the newspaper and checking out her apartment? Jimi and I will make visits to our two suspects from the past."

She wasn't sure she liked this plan. Though she appreciated the chance to forge ahead with her own investigation, she'd miss Crawford's experienced insights. Not wanting to be perceived as difficult, she accepted. "You're the boss."

"We have rooms at the Captain's Cove B&B. Meet us there in the parlor at ten o'clock."

She ended the call and joined Jake. Crawford had put her in charge, and she intended to be thorough, starting with the local detective. "How well did you know Phoebe?"

"Enough to say hi."

"Tell me about her. Did she live here all her life?"

He shook his head. "Phoebe moved to Astoria after graduating from University of Oregon three or four years ago. She interned at the *Sun*, working on both the print and online versions. It's a local paper but has been in business since the late 1800s and has a solid reputation. Joseph Rogers, aka Jolly Rogers, is the editor-in-chief. He's been at the paper for as long as I can remember. After her internship, he gave Phoebe a full-time job."

"Getting hired by a legitimate newspaper, even a small operation, is a coup." The outlets for responsible journalism were shrinking all the time. "What were her goals? Did she expect to stay here?"

"Not for long," he said. "Phoebe wrote a couple of articles that drew national attention. One on *The Goonies*. Hard to believe anybody remembers that movie or cares, but she wouldn't stop bragging. She also did an article on one of the kid stars, Ke Huy Quan, after he won his Oscar. I think she saw Astoria as a stepping stone to a bigger and better career."

"Ambitious." She wasn't surprised. In the note, Phoebe Conway had been lavishly praised and promised a scoop. The killer lured her to him by appealing to her ego. She and Jake paused outside the door to the *Sun*.

He grasped the handle but didn't open it. "Tabitha knew her better than I did."

"I'll talk to her," Skylar said, recalling how the Elvira-wannabe had drooled over Jake. She'd be less distracted talking to another woman. "You check with Quilling and make sure he isn't parading evidence in front of reporters. Find out if anybody else in the office saw the person who delivered the note to Phoebe."

"Got it." He yanked the glass door open.

Stepping inside the open bullpen with desks scattered amid Halloween decor, Skylar stared up at the black-and-orange streamers hanging from the ceiling. Tawdry and limp. She checked out the likely places for surveillance and saw no indication of hidden cameras. Under her breath, she said, "No security."

"What are they going to steal at a newspaper?" Jake mumbled back to her. "Words?"

Skylar approached the front counter. Though she'd met Tabitha before, she wanted to establish boundaries. In a practiced move, she flashed her FBI credentials. "Remember me? I'm Special Agent Gambel, and I have a few questions."

Though Tabitha nodded, her heavily lined eyes seemed to follow Jake as he went to the desk behind the yellow crime scene tape and spoke to Alan Quilling. Clearly disappointed, she turned back to Skylar. "Yes, ma'am. How can I help you?"

"I didn't notice any security cams at the front entrance."

"Nope. People just come and go as they please. It's my job to refer them to the right desk for placing ads. Or to a reporter who might cover an event they're hosting. Or an obit writer. They're supposed to sign in with me at the counter. Most of the time, they don't bother."

"That must make you angry."

"Not really. Sometimes, I just have to take a break. Or go to the little girl's room. Or run a quick errand. I figure if it's important, the person will wait for me or come back."

"Very practical," she said. "Did you see the person who left the note for Phoebe?"

Tabitha narrowed her eyes in a futile attempt to remember.

Then, she shrugged. "Sorry. When Quilling showed me the address, I remembered Phoebe waving the envelope around after lunch and asking who left it. I didn't remember then. Or now."

"You knew Phoebe better than most people. Tell me about her."

"Well, to start with, she was insanely pretty. Long, streaked blond hair that was always glossy and perfect. Great bod. She knew how to dress, you know, her clothes matched. Everything about her was exactly what my mother would adore." Tabitha hiccuped, a sob catching in her throat. "I can't believe she's dead."

"She must have had a lot of boyfriends."

"She dated a lot. A different guy every day of the week."

"Playing the field. Not ready to settle down. There wasn't anybody special? Had she recently had a breakup?"

"Oh, I get it." Tabitha gave a knowing wink. "You think some guy she was dating attacked her."

"What do you think?"

Tabitha drew her mouth into a small red circle outlined in black. "Maybe."

Skylar wasn't sure how much of Tabitha's info fell into the category of gossip and how much was truth. Didn't matter. She and Jake needed to track down all the boyfriends. At least to run them through NCIC and ViCAP to check for criminal records. "I'd appreciate if you'd write a list with full names, how long she dated them and anything else that might be pertinent."

"Like what?"

"Maybe they took Phoebe on vacation or bought her a special gift. Some guys just stand out from the rest."

"I know what you're saying, Special Agent." Tabitha drawled over Skylar's title. "You have a real badass job. Do you think I can get hired by the FBI?"

"It's a lot of work to get this job."

"Seriously? How hard could it be?"

Skylar didn't appreciate the implied insult. *How hard could it be?* "I have a law degree, worked as an assistant DA, graduated from Quantico and qualified as a Marine-level sharpshooter. I have a brown belt in karate, paramedic training and top-level security clearance." She finished her coffee and dropped the container into a trash can with a re-sounding thud. "Becoming a special agent isn't easy."

Chastised, Tabitha backed down. "That's not what it looks like on TV."

"Life seldom is."

The door to one of the offices against the back wall flung open with such emphasis that the half-wall-size window shud-dered. A gruff, heavy-shouldered man with kinky gray hair and thick black eyebrows stuck his head into the bullpen and barked. "Ahoy, Armstrong. Get your tail over here. Right now."

"Aye, aye." Jake motioned for her to join him. "Let's go meet Jolly Rogers. Managing editor of the *Astoria Sun*."

"Was he working here twenty years ago?'

"You bet. Rogers was a young reporter, probably in his thirties. Back then, he was married, had a seven-year-old kid." At the door to Rogers's office, he gestured for her to enter first, closed the door behind them, introduced her and asked, "What is it, sir?"

"This note came to our open forum for the online *Astoria Sun*. Could be your killer, trying to copycat the Lightkeeper from twenty years ago." Rogers turned his computer screen so they could read.

The first thing Skylar noticed was the signature line:

I rise from the night and the darkness. Call me Shadow-keeper.

As she'd suspected, he had named himself.

Chapter Eight

Shadowkeeper. Jake despised the comic book name. *Shadowkeeper*. *The Shadow*. It conjured up images of a supervillain in tights and a dark cape. This wasn't a game. The so-called Shadowkeeper wasn't special or clever. Murder should never be celebrated.

In the Shadowkeeper's first note to Phoebe Conway on her cell phone, the killer insinuated that she'd get what she deserved. A sick joke. Ironic. Phoebe surely believed she deserved fame and fortune. The Shadowkeeper—a narcissist like Skylar predicted—had something else in mind.

Jake stood beside Special Agent Gambel, close enough to smell the vanilla and citrus fragrance of her shampoo. When she stretched across the desk in Rogers's office to read the Shadowkeeper's post on the computer screen, the sleeve of her charcoal gray jacket brushed the plaid sleeve of his shirt. Instead of pulling back, he leaned toward her. Gazing down, he saw the black leather belt holster under her jacket. The lethal weapon contrasted her silky, cream-colored blouse. Without even trying, Special Agent Skylar Gambel tapped into dreams and desires he didn't know he had.

Jake read the Shadowkeeper's note on the screen:

Phoebe Conway got what was coming to her. I granted her the honor of being my first victim. She'll go down in history. Thousands of ghouls will read about her online and wonder why I selected her. Too bad she won't be around to write a column for herself.

Some clues for you, Armstrong. I work alone. I hear no voices. And I serve no master.

I rise from the night and the darkness. Call me Shadow-keeper.

Rogers dragged his thick fingers through his curly gray hair. His voice grated like a cement mixer. "I always knew we'd hear from that bastard again."

Jake pointed out the obvious. "You don't think it's a copycat."

"Don't know. But I never believed a curse from a librarian would make him quit killing." Rogers's jaw tensed and his eyes darted beneath his thick black brows. For a long moment, the gruff old man looked scared. His gaze flicked around the incredibly messy office and landed on one of the few photographs on the bookshelves—a picture of a boy in a Little League baseball uniform for the Astoria Otters. Rogers slammed both fists down onto his cluttered desktop, causing the computer screen to jump. "He'll never stop."

Jake understood Rogers's anger and his fear. But not his logic. The Lightkeeper had ended his serial killer spree. For twenty years, there had been no murders attributed to him.

Skylar turned toward Jake with a question in her eyes. "He mentioned you, Detective. Challenged you."

"Could be somebody I've arrested or ticketed. Somebody carrying a grudge." He never claimed to be the most popular guy in town. "Some people just don't like cops."

"Some people are wrong." Her green-eyed gaze studied him like an X-ray machine, trying to see beneath the surface. "The note says he works alone, doesn't hear voices and serves no master. Why does he think this is a clue?"

"Those characteristics are markedly different from the Lightkeeper," Jake said. "He's telling us that he isn't the same killer from the past."

"Teasing us," Rogers growled. "Pointing us in the wrong direction."

Skylar kept her focus on Jake. "You studied the Lightkeeper."

"When I was ten," he reminded her.

"I'd still like to hear your insights. Give me a quick description."

"A loner, one of those guys who fades into the woodwork. Claimed to be on a mission and believed people would thank him for ridding the world of these flawed women. He referenced a high priestess who whispered in his ear. She demanded sacrifices."

"A contradiction," Skylar said. "He believes his victims deserve punishment. But also thinks they are pure enough to be sacrificial lambs."

"The Lightkeeper never pretended to make rational sense," he said. "I can show you profiles from the FBI and other psychologists. After analyzing his communications, they were pretty sure he suffered from schizophrenia. He experienced hallucinations and heard voices. His condition used to be called split personality."

"DID," she said, "Dissociative Identity Disorder."

His amateur investigations and the opinions of experts had steered him toward that diagnosis. Not that he understood how DID worked. Jake wasn't a psychologist, didn't comprehend brain chemistry. All he could say for certain was that the Lightkeeper was driven to kill and imagined himself to be part of a greater cause. In his head, he heard instructions from a priestess or witch who didn't really exist and, therefore, wasn't—thank God—Dagmar's mom.

"This online note is a trick," Rogers said. "He's trying to confuse Armstrong."

"Doing a damned good job," the detective muttered. He respected the editor's opinion. Rogers's byline topped many of the articles from twenty years ago. At one point, the Lightkeeper sent his follow-up note and cassette to Rogers's home along with a threat to his wife and young son. "But why me? I'm just a cop. Not a brilliant detective. Why would the Shadowkeeper call me out?"

"You're a threat, and he doesn't want to get caught." Rogers threw his arms in the air. "He got away with murder before. Thinks he can do it again. Thinks he's smarter than we are."

"Is he?" Skylar asked.

Rogers glared at her. "Where's your boss? Where's Crawford? He should be here."

"Supervisory Special Agent Crawford is my partner. He's pursuing a different direction in our investigation." She followed up with another question. "Why do you think the Shadowkeeper killed a woman who worked at the *Sun*?"

"To make sure he gets full media coverage. That's what he did the first time around. Kept sending notes and tapes. Scared the hell out of me." He lumbered across his office and stood at the half-glass wall where someone—probably Tabitha—had painted a Halloween vampire. Under lowered brows, Rogers scanned from left to right, trying to see a shadow that wasn't there.

Jake noticed Ty McKenna, a reporter he'd gone to high school with, leaning against his desk and staring back at Rogers's office.

The old man continued, "The Lightkeeper threatened me and my family. I sent my wife and my son, Bradley, to live with her mother in Houston until I was certain the killing spree was finally over. And that, my friends, was the beginning of the end of my marriage."

Even as a kid, Jake remembered the divorce as epic. Rogers's wife, a stunning woman, had taken every opportunity to bash him in furious public arguments while being careful that her rage didn't interfere with her sole custody of their son. Hoping to divert the subject, he asked, "Didn't you write a book about the Lightkeeper?"

"Never finished it." Rogers staggered to the swivel chair behind his desk, sank into it and exhaled heavily. "Maybe it's time for me to do that—write the damn book. Or I could retire, sell my house and cruise up and down the coast on my fishing trawler, the *Jolly Rogers*."

"I didn't know you were a sailor," Jake said.

"Not a sailboat, matey. This old pirate has a twenty-eight-foot trawler with a diesel motor. There's a berth in the hull and a galley in the cabin for cooking fish I catch myself. The boat's nineteen years old but in good shape. A gift to myself because I don't have family to worry about. My ex-wife just got married for the third time and moved to Paris. France, not Texas, her home state."

"What about your son?"

"Bradley and I never really got back together after the divorce. Too bad. I would have been a great dad. We talk on the phone. I send him cash, and he occasionally visits but hasn't lived here since high school. I thought, maybe, after his mom got married again, he'd reach out."

"I'd like to read your notes," Skylar said. "For your book."

He nodded. "I'll email you the file."

Jake watched as she rearranged her features into a no-nonsense expression. "Sir, I need to know where you were last night between eleven and three."

Rogers jolted upright in his chair. His simmering frustration exploded. "What the hell! Am I a damn suspect?"

Jake should have seen the eruption coming and put a lid on it. Should have done his job, damn it, he should have been the one to ask for an alibi because he had a relationship with Rogers that could have encouraged cooperation.

"I need to know," she said, "for the purpose of eliminating you from our investigation. Where were you?"

"I went to bed at half past eleven after I heard the weather report on the news. Before you ask, I'll tell you that I live alone. No one to verify."

"Home alone with no witness. Correct?"

"You got it." He sank back into his chair, causing the springs to creak. "Are we done?"

Belatedly efficient, Jake stepped up. "We're going to need Phoebe's employment records and any documentation you have on her. Also, we'll track the IP that sent the Shadow-keeper's message to the *Sun*."

Rogers gestured toward the bullpen and front desk. "Tabitha can take care of the background info. Get McKenna to help. He dated Phoebe."

"And if we have more questions—"

"I'll be here. Close the damn door on your way out."

Jake and Skylar stood together outside Rogers's office. When she tucked a strand of hair behind her ear, the overhead lights glistened on her glossy mane. The flush in her cheeks showed the tension from her confrontation. In a low voice, she said, "He's a suspect."

"Yes."

"We should keep him under surveillance tonight."

"I'll arrange for a stakeout."

He turned his gaze away from her and into the cluttered bullpen.

Ty McKenna stood with arms folded across his chest, waiting to be questioned. Jake had always thought McKenna was too eager. During high school track meets, he always jumped the gun.

"As for Quilling," she said, "he needs to wait for the experts before trying to figure out who sent that email to the newspaper."

"When will they be in touch?"

"Soon," she promised. "The FBI's cybercrimes division is brilliant at manipulating the internet, and they'll keep your forensic guy in the loop, maybe teach him a thing or two about investigating. The cyber-detectives can also scan Phoebe's social media pages and her newspaper articles. She was a public person, which means she probably left a deep, wide, colorful trail."

"With so many paths to research, we're going to need more officers working the case." When Skylar had been questioning Rogers about his alibi, Jake realized they had many other people to interview, including Phoebe's friends, acquaintances and—most important—her enemies. "Chief Kim will have her hands full, coordinating assignments."

"Has she already notified Phoebe's parents?"

"First thing she did. They're flying in from Houston tomorrow."

"That's where Rogers's wife is from. Any connection?"

"We'll see."

She shot a hard-edged glare at McKenna. "Let's get started with the ex-boyfriend. It's your turn to take the lead."

They picked their way through the desks in the bullpen until they stood in front of Ty McKenna—a slim, tall hipster in a flannel vest, a brown pinstriped shirt and a neck scarf in the classic Burberry pattern. His close-cropped black hair matched his carefully cultivated five o'clock shadow. His classy Movado wristwatch screamed money, an accurate description for anybody in the McKenna family.

After Jake introduced Skylar, he directed McKenna toward the break room at the far edge of the bullpen so they could have privacy. When the swinging door closed, the small room went silent except for the hum of a space heater. The smell of old coffee and stale doughnuts hung in the air. The three of them sat around a square table.

Jake asked, "When was the last time you saw Phoebe?"

"Yesterday in the office." With his elbows planted on the plastic tabletop, McKenna hunched over like a praying mantis. "She was all smug and superior. Like she had a secret. Which, I guess, she did. Well, damn, I should have paid more attention."

Jake heard the tension in McKenna's tone and a note of guilt. "You and Phoebe were dating earlier this year."

"Listen, there's something I should tell you—both of you. I've made some mistakes in my life and don't want you to think I'm hiding anything."

When Jake gave him the nod, McKenna blurted, "I have a criminal record. When I was in grad school, I had a drinking problem. I got a DUI and was convicted on two charges of disturbing the peace. Bar fights. Broke a couple of bottles. Threw some weak punches. This girl got a bloody nose."

Jake translated: McKenna hit a woman and now his ex-girlfriend was murdered. Not looking good. He sensed feelings of revulsion coming from Skylar. Her slender fingers knotted together on the tabletop, and he had no doubt that she could effectively punish McKenna if need be. As she'd mentioned, she was Quantico-trained. A brown belt in karate.

"What happened?" Jake asked.

"Nothing. She didn't press charges. I got off with a fine and community service."

"At the time, where were you living?"

"Seattle, going to U-Dub. I was a dumb ass kid, but I got my act together." He lifted his chin and made direct eye contact. "Four years, three months and ten days ago, I joined AA. I've been sober ever since."

"Congratulations," Jake said, and he meant it. Going straight wasn't easy. "Let's get back to Phoebe."

"We were inevitable." McKenna paused for emphasis. "I was almost forced to date her. We worked together for three years. We were good reporters, competitive in a positive way. She appeared on the Portland TV news four times. I had seven special segments."

"What else can you tell me about your relationship?"

McKenna's head drooped, and he stared down at his hands on the tabletop. "Like I said. Inevitable. Me and Phoebe... We both have apartments in the same house. Made it easy when I said your place or mine. She was just down the hall."

Too close for comfort.

Chapter Nine

Skylar leaned back in the uncomfortable plastic chair in the break room and stretched her legs, watching while Jake conducted his interview with Ty McKenna. The wealthy, cool hipster ticked all the relevant boxes when it came to being a suspect. Number one, he had a record for being drunk and disorderly, even though he was now sober. Two, he had dated Phoebe, and they'd broken up. Three, he and the victim were competitors. Four, they lived in the same building, which was, for a possible stalker, a bonus.

However, McKenna also had a solid alibi. He told Jake that he spent last night at the Sand Bar, a local tavern, where he was the designated driver for four friends. He dropped off the last drinker after the bar closed at two in the morning. Should be easy enough to verify.

Though McKenna sounded confident and showed the aforementioned competitive streak when he talked about beating his drunk buddies in a darts game, Skylar read a different story from his microexpressions and gestures. McKenna repeatedly touched his nose, which made her think of Pinocchio. His gaze flickered. And he stroked the stubble on his chin, hiding his mouth and holding back lies.

She definitely doubted his truthfulness when the topic shifted back to his relationship with Phoebe. According to

McKenna, he dumped her because she was too possessive and demanding. He called her a diva. Self-important. A mean girl.

Skylar suspected the same description applied to Ty McKenna. *A mean girl despite his gender.* Especially when he told them that the renovated mansion where they both lived belonged to his parents. He'd advised them to evict Phoebe when she was late with her rent. A spiteful move. Skylar didn't like this guy or trust him but couldn't be sure he was a killer.

Jake was a smooth interrogator. He did a good job of drawing McKenna out and letting him talk enough to reveal the ugly side of his polished personality. The interview ended with the two men shaking hands and McKenna promising they'd get together and hang out. He didn't notice how Jake wiped the palm of his hand on his khakis, as if to erase the slimy contact.

McKenna disengaged from them, saying he needed to check with Rogers about a piece he wanted to write, then he'd meet them at the six-apartment renovated mansion where he and Phoebe both had lived.

After they left the break room, Tabitha handed Jake a legal-size envelope filled with employment documents and columns written by Phoebe Conway, which Rogers had told her to compile. She leaned close to Jake. Too close. If he wanted, he could have peeked down her low-cut black sweater. Instead, he averted his gaze, which pleased Skylar more than it should. Not only was he great to look at, but he was poised and professional.

She kept her opinions to herself. Working with Jake would be acceptable. Anything more was not.

Before they left the *Sun*, they talked to Quilling who peeked at her with big, round, brown eyes like a naughty puppy. *A mutt who's mishandled evidence.* She stayed aloof, reminding him that she was the boss. Still, she had to admit that Quilling's excitement about working with the FBI cybercrime division endeared him to her and made her want to scratch behind his ears.

OUTSIDE, DAYLIGHT HAD faded into a gloomy night. Skylar settled into the passenger seat of the SUV and peered through the windshield. Jake had advised her about the fog and clouds causing poor visibility, and the October weather proved him right. The streetlights barely made a difference. The shadows deepened and diffused.

Mysterious and creepy, the Shadowkeeper had chosen an apt name for himself.

Leaving the business district and the docks, they headed toward the residential area of this town built on hillsides. The visit to Phoebe's apartment would help establish a timeline. According to Tabitha—who might not be the most accurate source—Phoebe had left work last night at six. If she arrived at the Cape Meares Lighthouse at midnight and the drive took an hour and a half, that left four and a half hours unaccounted for. Skylar wanted to fill in that blank.

Jake cruised through Astoria with the familiarity of a native who doesn't need street signs to know where he's going. He parked the Explorer at the curb outside a three-story gingerbread-trimmed Victorian mansion, typical of many of the renovated homes dotting the hillsides. Though decently maintained on a corner lot with landscaped hedges, shrubs, a red-leafed maple and a persimmon tree full of plump orange fruits, the mini-mansion showed signs of wear. Could have used a paint job. The roof above the porch was saggy. The house and grounds were poorly illuminated by a corner streetlight swaddled in fog.

An unwarranted sense of foreboding rose up inside her as she studied the face of the building. Light glowed from several windows, including a narrow casement on the third floor.

With a shudder, Skylar recalled ghostly stories about evil creatures locked in the attic and only released at the full moon. Her skin prickled, and her shoulders tensed. She shook off the chill. *Don't be absurd.* This wasn't the home of the Addams family. Her mom, dressed as Morticia Addams, would not step through the front door to welcome them into her lair.

She glanced over at Jake who stood on the sidewalk beside her—tall, protective and intensely masculine. Being with him made her feel safe, and she liked the un-feminist sensation that would have gotten her laughed out of Quantico. No matter how pleasant it might be to snuggle up against that broad chest, she didn't need a bodyguard. In a level tone, she said, "McKenna gave me the master key, but I think we should wait for him before we go inside."

"Can't waste much time," Jake said. "It's eight forty-five, and we're meeting SSA Crawford and Jimi Kim at the B&B at ten. Before that, I need to check in with Chief Kim on the status of our investigation."

"We'll give McKenna five minutes." He was probably pitching Rogers an article about the intimate details of his relationship with the Shadowkeeper's first victim. Nothing like a grand tragedy to draw in readers. Though some reporters were brilliant and even heroic, she saw their breed as the jackals of crime investigation, skulking around to pick the bones of the victims. "He's an annoying person."

"Still, I've got to hand it to the guy. I didn't know about his drinking problem. I respect him for getting sober."

They approached the wrought iron fence surrounding the property. A decorative sign by the gate gave the street number and the name of the mansion: Agate House.

Skylar looked forward to searching Phoebe's apartment. Decor, possessions and housekeeping habits revealed a great deal about people. "I wonder if she was tidy or a hoarder."

"I'm guessing she has quality stuff. Tasteful. Classy. She dressed too fancy for my taste but always looked good. Had a pair of those high heels with the red soles."

"I want to talk to the other people who live here. I'd like to clarify the timeline, find out when she got home and when she left. If the Shadowkeeper was stalking her, he might have visited."

"We still haven't decided if the Shadowkeeper is a man," he reminded her.

"Obviously, we don't have a description. But we know the Shadowkeeper managed to carry Phoebe to the winding staircase. Whether she was unconscious or struggling like crazy, lifting her required strength. Sure, a woman could have done it. A big, muscular woman."

"Like Dagmar," he interjected.

"We'll keep an open mind, but it's likely that the killer is a man in good physical condition."

"If you don't mind, I'd rather interview the other people living here and leave the search through Phoebe's apartment to you. Pawing through other people's stuff isn't my thing. Makes me feel like a Peeping Tom."

"Not me." She grinned. "Snooping is one of my guilty pleasures. Ever since I was a kid and found my mom's stash of sexy romance novels hidden behind the towels on the lowest shelf of the bathroom linen closet, I've liked poking into other people's secrets."

He held open the gate, and she strolled up the flagstone path to a covered porch with slate blue trim and bannisters. Before she could knock, the heavy front door swung open, framing Ty McKenna in a vintage peacoat. He gasped for breath.

"You're winded," she said. "Have you been running?"

"Drove right here. Parked in back. Came through the rear door." He swept open the door. "Please come in."

Again, she had the impression he was being less than truthful. McKenna might have rushed here ahead of them to slip into Phoebe's apartment and remove an incriminating piece of evidence.

The front vestibule held a row of average-size mailboxes and two lockers for large packages. Beyond a door that locked was a large hallway with a dining room on one side and a TV room with an extra-large flat-screen on the other. The kitchen was probably in the back.

"No apartments on the first floor," McKenna said. "Upstairs are four singles and two family-size with two bedrooms. No children. No pets."

"Does anyone live on the top floor?" she asked.

"There's one apartment in the attic. The guy who lives there has been at Agate House for thirteen years, ever since he moved to Astoria." McKenna climbed the carved oak staircase that bisected the first floor. "You probably know him, Jake. He teaches science at the high school. Robert Pierce."

"Pyro Pierce," Jake said. "That was his nickname because he was always blowing things up in chem lab."

Another eccentric detail. She paused on the landing. "Which apartment belonged to Phoebe?"

"Number three." He gestured to the right where a mint green door with a gold number three awaited. "It's the second-best suite with two bedrooms, a bathroom, kitchenette and a view of the street."

"Which is the best?"

"Mine, of course." He preened.

"Is this the only door to her apartment?"

"That would be against fire regs," he said. "A French door opens onto the porch roof, and there's a ladder down from there."

"Good to know." She glanced over her shoulder at Jake. "I'll look around in Phoebe's place. You question the other residents."

"I'm on it." He ascended a narrower staircase to the third

floor, apparently choosing to start his interrogations with the pyromaniac science teacher.

Skylar crossed the threshold into Phoebe Conway's former residence. The dead woman's home screamed with brilliant colors and patterns. *Look at me. Notice me.* A gold clock in a glass case chimed at the quarter hour. The potpourri scent of lavender mingled with the sweet aroma from a bouquet of fresh red roses. High ceilings and tall windows created a spacious feeling. The feminine living room stretched into a small galley kitchen. An open bottle of red from a Willamette Valley winery stood beside a half-full glass and a carryout container from a bistro. The food and drink filled in a blank on the timeline. Phoebe had picked up dinner last night and brought it home, which probably filled in another hour in the missing four and a half.

"Do I need to stay here while you poke around?" McKenna asked.

She didn't want to give him a chance to return to his apartment until she'd checked it out. "It's best if you stay." She didn't give a reason why. "Does the furniture belong to Phoebe?"

"Yeah, she brought her own stuff. Kind of picky that way."

Having recently moved to Portland, Skylar appreciated Phoebe's taste and orderly decor…until she entered the second bedroom that served as a home office. File folders, printouts, notebooks and reference material scattered across an L-shaped desk that also held a laptop and a computer with an extra-large screen. The color printer had a table all its own.

Skylar slipped on a pair of nitrile gloves before she started shuffling through the papers on the desk. Most of the documents related to the Lightkeeper's Curse Murders from twenty years ago. Obviously, Phoebe had been prepping to write an article after she received the note from the mystery person who summoned her to the lighthouse. How long did this research take? Two hours? Three? The precise time could be verified when the FBI cybercrime experts dumped the memory from her computer. Her electronics would show where she was at the given times. Time-stamped listings from her personal phone would indicate who she'd been talking to and what she'd been doing before her midnight appointment.

Unlike the rest of the apartment where the wall hangings had been selected by color and content, the office featured a cluster of plaques, citations and awards—testimony to Phoebe Conway's success in her field and the pride she took in her accomplishments. Pride or hubris? It could be argued that Phoebe's ambition caused her lack of caution and led to her murder.

Wrong! Skylar knew better than to blame the victim.

The rest of the wall space in the office was chockful of photographs. Some framed and others stuck onto cork bulletin boards. The majority of the pictures featured a smiling, beautiful Phoebe and a male companion.

Scanning slowly, she noticed very few pictures of other women. An indication that she had few female friends. Or maybe she didn't value their friendship enough to take a picture together. With a frown, Skylar once again dismissed her snap judgment. If she'd put together a collage of her own life, there would only be one close girlfriend she'd stayed in touch with since seventh grade. Growing up with two brothers put her in contact with more guys than gals. And her coworkers at the FBI were predominantly male. Nothing wrong with that.

Still, Phoebe's wall of men might have a deeper meaning. She'd posted these pictures near her workspace. Maybe to remind herself of her many conquests... The way a big game hunter hung trophies on his walls.

She spotted several of McKenna. Several others of a

familiar-looking face who might be a celebrity. Another photo caught her eye. Phoebe had wrapped both arms around a tall, skinny guy with floppy brown hair and round glasses.

Surprised, Skylar stared at this odd and unexpected clue. The man in the picture with Phoebe was Alan Quilling, the head of APD's forensics unit.

Chapter Ten

Though Jake had to duck under an exposed beam in the third-floor attic apartment at Agate House, the space didn't feel cramped to him. The horizontal square footage of the open floor plan stretched from the front to the back of the building, plenty of room to roam. Vertically? Not so much.

The mansard roof was supported by arched beams, some of which weren't much taller than six feet high at the outer edges. They were too low for him; he stood six feet six inches in his bare feet. The many built-in shelves held books, papers, artwork, plastic models of body parts and weird equipment probably used in experiments by Jake's former high school science teacher, Robert Pierce. Two side-by-side windows at either end were designed to provide light during the day. On the western side of the apartment were long, wide dormers with shelves for dozens of leafy green plants and fragrant herbs.

Jake had taken only one chem class with Pierce, who must have started teaching right after college and was only six or seven years older. He looked much the same as he did back then. Short and solidly built, he wore his dark brown hair—still without a thread of gray—in a long ponytail. Pyro Pierce was known for riding his cross-country bike to school.

"I remember you, Armstrong. Advanced chem, senior year, A-plus student." Pierce pushed up his glasses onto the bridge of his hawklike nose. "You spent a lot of time figuring out the physics behind Batman's gadgets and Iron Man's suit."

Nerdy but true. "My favorite superheroes. They weren't aliens or magically transformed by a laboratory accident."

"Heroes you could identify with." Pierce gestured toward a kitchen table and two chairs at the edge of a kitchenette. "Would you like a cup of herbal tea? I have organic apple blossom. And fresh-baked banana bread to go with."

"Thanks, but no." The bread smelled great. Jake was tempted to sit and chat but needed to stay focused. "Are you aware of Phoebe Conway's murder?"

"She lived downstairs." Pierce cocked his head to one side. "That's why you're here. Am I right? You're a police detective. A whole different breed of hero."

"I wouldn't say that." In his real-life adventures as a cop, he never expected glamor or applause. Jake fumbled for words, couldn't decide exactly what perspective to take. Pierce might be a useful witness but was also a possible suspect. "How well did you know her?"

"Casually. We'd bump into each other on the stairs and say hello. She wasn't a bad neighbor, and I hope you won't think I'm sexist if I say she was *not* unpleasant to look at." He glanced up and to the right, as if conjuring a memory of Skylar's attributes. "Her body was toned but not athletic. Her symmetrical features made her pretty in a conventional way. Fluffy hair like an Afghan hound. And she had a slight but appealing hint of Texas accent."

"Negatives?" Jake asked.

"She was haughty and ambitious, which aren't necessarily bad traits. I'm all for goal setting." He chuckled. "Phoebe was a fan of *The Goonies*. Gotta like that."

"Did you ever ask her out?"

Pierce frowned. "Dating a woman in the building seemed like a bad idea because it could lead to uncomfortable meetings in the hallways after the probable breakup. Besides, Phoebe never lacked for male companionship, including Ty McKenna. Have you spoken to him?"

"You bet." The telescope near the front window caught Jake's attention. He made the trek across several mismatched throw rugs on the hardwood floor to take a closer look. "What part of the night sky can you see from here?"

"We're facing northwest, so I'm looking at Cassiopeia, Pegasus and the Andromeda galaxy. I prefer taking the telescope to the roof to study astronomy during celestial events like meteor showers or an eclipse of the moon if the fog doesn't get in the way. Some people say we can see the northern lights from Astoria. But I've never found that to be true."

Pierce stepped up beside him and peered through the window glass. When they'd first arrived at Agate House, Jake had seen a silhouette from this upstairs window. "You have a good vantage point to watch the comings and goings of people who live here."

"I certainly do. You showed up twelve minutes ago and were accompanied by an attractive brunette in a conservative suit. I'm guessing she carries a sidearm. A lady cop?"

"An FBI special agent."

"Score one for me," Pierce said. "I'm not a snoop, but I like to figure stuff out."

That characterization sounded right to Jake. A science teacher would naturally be inquisitive. "Did you notice anything unusual about Phoebe's visitors?"

"Like what? Were they obvious ax murderers or drooling psychotics? Honestly, Jake, this interview would move along more quickly if you asked direct questions. There's no point in being subtle."

"What do you mean?"

"I have an alibi," he said.

"Okay."

"From what I've heard, Phoebe was killed on Cape Disappointment at about midnight. At the time, I was…occupied. A friend spent the night." He gestured toward the only enclosed portion of his apartment, which had to be where the bedroom and bathroom were located. "Actually, I think you know my lady."

He knew a lot of people. Astoria was a small town. "Does she have a name?"

"Dagmar Burke."

Jake shook his head. *Cousin Dagmar. Of course. Why not?* They were both single, close to the same age and both a little weird. But trustworthy. Mentally, he crossed Pyro Pierce off the list of suspects. "You and Dagmar, huh?"

"Precisely. Now, tell me what you're looking for. Not general traits, but something more specific."

More scientific. "According to our evidence, the killer knew Phoebe and was familiar with the Lightkeeper's Curse Murders from twenty years ago. He might have been watching her or stalking."

"He? Are you sure the killer is male?"

Jake had to be careful not to divulge specifics about an ongoing investigation. Skylar had gone ballistic when Quilling showed the phone photo of the killer's note. If Jake started sharing conclusions about their murderer or the murder scene, she'd explode. "Let's talk about stalking. Have you noticed a stranger hanging around the neighborhood? Or a vehicle that didn't belong here?"

"Matter of fact, I have. There was a car, a black sedan with tinted windows. It's been parked along the street three or four times in the past few weeks."

A strange car might mean nothing, or it might lead to the killer. The Son of Sam serial killer, David Berkowitz, was apprehended because of a parking ticket near one of the crime scenes. "What else can you tell me about this car?"

"I don't know the make or model."

Of course not. Pierce wasn't a car guy. "Are you still riding your bike everywhere?"

"Keeps me in shape." Pierce bristled. "That doesn't mean I'm opposed to other forms of transportation. I bought a used van for hauling groceries and packing supplies for camping trips, but I prefer my mountain bike for everything else. My Carbonjack is a beauty and cost a whole lot more than the gas-guzzling vehicle."

Jake dragged him back to the topic. "About this black sedan…"

"I know who it belongs to," Pierce said. "The driver wasn't in the vehicle, but I was riding past on my bike and looked in the window. There was a decal with a skull and crossbones on the dashboard."

"The Jolly Roger." The symbol associated with the editor-in-chief of the *Astoria Sun*. Rogers had no alibi. "Anything else?"

"A folded copy of the *Sun* on the passenger seat. And a bumper sticker that says, My Other Car is a Fishing Trawler."

It had to be Rogers. "Thanks, you've been a great help."

"Come back anytime, Armstrong. The world needs more heroes."

In the hallway with the door to Pierce's apartment closed, Jake leaned against the wall and closed his eyes, waiting for his random thoughts to sort themselves into logic. Though he was supposed to interrogate the other residents of Agate House—two couples and a single female—he needed to act on this lead.

Rogers had been stalking Phoebe. He had no alibi for last night, which made him the number one suspect. If he was the murderer, he might be starting a string of serial killings. In his note, the Shadowkeeper said Phoebe was his *first victim*.

Obvious conclusion: Jake needed to get Rogers under surveillance as soon as possible.

He charged down the staircase to the second floor where Skylar and McKenna had just exited Phoebe's apartment. Maintaining calm instead of the urgency churning in his gut, he said, "I need to speak to you immediately, Agent Gambel."

A frown pinched her forehead between her sculpted brows. "Something wrong?"

"We need to talk. Now."

"First, we'll accompany McKenna to his apartment."

He gritted his teeth and fell into step behind her and McKenna. They were wasting time. Another person might be killed.

At the apartment in the rear of the house, McKenna unlocked the door and stepped inside in front of them. He tried to shut it, but Skylar braced her shoulder against the door.

Standing behind her, Jake couldn't see what was happening. Before he could react, she made her move. Faster than a speeding bullet. Equally lethal. She whipped her jacket out of the way, drew her sidearm and dropped into a shooter's stance.

On the other side of a coffee table, McKenna had picked up a gun of his own. He held it away from his body, not aiming but lying flat on the palm of his hand.

"Drop the weapon," Skylar ordered in a voice laced with steel.

"Whatever you say. Don't shoot."

Wisely, he chose not to fight. McKenna lowered his gun to the table, stepped back and raised his hands.

Skylar didn't relax her stance.

"I've got it," Jake said as he picked up the gun—a pricey, compact Springfield Armory. "Got a handgun permit?"

"It belongs to my dad."

"Hold out your arms."

Unwisely, McKenna chose to resist. "What if I don't want to?"

Tired of the whining from this entitled jerk, Jake switched into his military persona. Rough. Tough. And straight as an arrow. They needed to act, to move fast and make sure Rogers was under surveillance. "Do it now."

Surprised, McKenna obeyed.

Quick and aggressive, he frisked McKenna and turned to his partner. "No other weapons."

She holstered her Glock. "I wonder if he's on some kind of extended probation. Prohibited from dealing with other scumbags. Restricted from carrying lethal weapons."

Jake had another concern. "Why is this gun lying around unsecured? It should be put away, locked in a safe."

"I loaned it to Phoebe," McKenna said. "Before I let you into the house, I went into her apartment, grabbed the gun and brought it here."

"You thought Phoebe needed a handgun," Jake said. "Why?"

"She worried that somebody was following her."

She couldn't have been talking about Rogers, her boss. She knew him. "And why did you steal the gun away from her apartment?"

"Appearances," Skylar said. "He didn't want us to know he had a gun. Right?"

"I suppose."

She reached into her purse and pulled out handcuffs. "You have a choice. Cooperate and do exactly as I say. Or I can arrest you for the obstruction of an ongoing murder investigation."

He stamped his foot like an angry hipster toddler. "I haven't done anything wrong."

"Obstruction it is." She nodded to Jake and said, "Turn him around so I can snap on the cuffs."

McKenna dodged around him and got up in Skylar's face. He jabbed his forefinger at her chest. "I've had enough, lady. You can't order me around."

He'd gone from unwise to flat-out stupid. Jake could have warned him not to get pushy with a fed. Or he could have taken McKenna down in a flash. But he waited to see what Skylar would do next.

She didn't disappoint. Skylar grabbed McKenna's wrist, pulled him off balance and kicked his leg out from under him. In seconds, the fashionable jerk was flat on his belly with Skylar looking down at him. "You're lucky you didn't touch me. I would have charged you with assaulting a federal officer. Do you agree to cooperate?"

McKenna forced himself to his knees. Grudgingly, he said, "I'll do what you say."

"Don't go anywhere tonight. Oh, and I'll be taking this pretty little gun."

"Like I told you, it belongs to my father. He's not going to be happy about this."

"Believe me when I say this, McKenna." Her lips curled in a glacial grin. "I don't care."

They descended the staircase and went through the vestibule and onto the porch where she turned to face him. "Lucky for McKenna, he has an alibi."

"So does Pierce, the science teacher in the third-floor apartment." Jake winced. "He spent the night with my cousin Dagmar."

"Madame Librarian?"

"But that's not the important thing. Pierce noticed a strange car outside Agate House. A black sedan had been there several times in the last few weeks."

"A stalker," she said. "Did he get a license plate?"

"Better. He peeked in the car window and saw a Jolly

Roger decal. A bumper sticker said, My Other Car is a Fishing Trawler."

"Rogers."

For the first time, she gave him a genuine, natural, spectacular smile. In the glow from the porch light, her long, auburn hair glistened, and her green eyes shimmered. Her lips parted, showing off a row of perfect white teeth.

He swallowed hard and forced himself to speak coherently. "I'll get the surveillance under way."

"Good work, Jake."

This might be the first time she'd used his given name. He'd graduated from the generic *detective* or *Armstrong*. "Thank you, Skylar."

Leaning into the shadows on the porch, she wrapped her arms around his torso for a hug. Her slender body pressed against his chest. He draped his arms over her shoulders and gently squeezed, imagining the sound of their hearts beating in harmony.

Their brief contact—less than five seconds—wasn't strictly professional, but he'd forgotten about his image or credibility. His mind filled with ideas about further intimacy. Maybe a kiss. Maybe more. He wanted Skylar beside him in his bed.

Chapter Eleven

With a name like Captain's Cove B&B, Skylar expected a nautical theme in the renovated Edwardian mansion, and she wasn't disappointed. The wallpaper in her room had an anchor design, and a dark blue fishing net draped artistically on the wall by the window. Kitschy but somewhat charming, not unlike foggy Astoria itself.

She never could have prepared herself for this setting that included twenty-year-old serial killings, curses, Halloween decor, a pregnant police chief and a tall, handsome detective. Her first assignment as a special agent presented a surprising challenge—one she meant to solve.

Her meeting in the downstairs parlor was scheduled for half an hour from now, enough time for a shower. She peeled off her slim leather hip holster, jacket, trousers, underwear and silky blouse, tossing each item onto the pale blue duvet. She'd hustled to arrive earlier than SSA Crawford so she could lay claim to the best bedroom. Her experience with road trips—while working as a lawyer and as an FBI analyst—taught her that the early bird gets the king-size bed, a spacious bathroom and the best view. From her window, she could see the one-hundred-twenty-five-foot-tall Astoria Column atop Coxcomb Hill.

Naked, she carried her Glock 19, still in the holster, into the bathroom and placed the weapon gently on a fluffy blue towel on the tiled countertop. She pulled her hair up on top of her head in a high ponytail and turned on the shower. In renovated homes like this one, the supply of hot water didn't come with a guarantee. The smart move was to grab a shower before Crawford got here. On their first out-of-Portland assignment together, she didn't know whether he was a shower hog or practitioner of the quickie. She suspected the former. His Silver Fox nickname suggested proper grooming.

The spray gushed, and the steam created a pleasantly warm fog as she stepped under the showerhead to rinse away a clammy layer of nervous sweat. Her perspiration hadn't resulted from physical activity. Her only exertion had been to sweep McKenna off his high-top lace-up boots. But her tension had been off the chart.

Luckily, her instincts had been right when she decided to ignore Jake's conflict of interest and partner up with him. He'd proved himself to be an able backup in the confrontation with McKenna and the earlier interrogation. She envied his overwhelming height and size that made him naturally intimidating. Not to mention the growl in his voice when angered. But he was more than a muscular sidekick. Jake was...so much more.

The pellets of hot water rained down and massaged her shoulders. Actually, Jake was nothing like a sidekick. More of a leading man. Smart, intuitive and motivated, his information moved Rogers from a benign position as a former victim and present-day witness to being *numero uno* suspect.

In spite of her unusual skills at reading character, she hadn't considered Rogers to be dangerous when they first met. He was all bluster and no bite. When he spoke of the Lightkeeper, he looked and sounded afraid. Intimidated. Still threatened after all these years.

But Jake had seen another side. She approved of his perceptiveness, his intelligence and...his wide shoulders. Every time she followed him along the sidewalk, she admired the way his upper body tapered to a lean torso and a truly fine bottom. An unintentional moan escaped her lips and echoed behind the shower curtain. Being hugged by Jake on the porch of McKenna's house, being held, even for a few seconds, felt incredible.

It had been a long time since she'd been in a real relationship.

Memory spiraled through her. During her summer vacation before her senior year in college, she was engaged to be married, preoccupied with planning the wedding, finding the perfect dress, selecting colors, flowers, bands and bridesmaids. The girly-girl role wasn't her natural style, but she played the role, dressing up and flashing her diamond ring because she thought she'd found the ideal mate.

She'd been so very wrong. He'd been a cheater who lied about everything, even her engagement ring with the phony diamonds and rubies. Her dreams were severed like a machete slashed through a four-tier wedding cake, and she vowed to keep a protective distance between herself and potential leading men like Jake. She wouldn't get carried away. Never again. Jake Armstrong was a friend and coworker, nothing more.

While she lathered her breasts, she remembered how enthusiastic he'd been about the progress of their case. Eagerly, he assumed the responsibility for communication with Chief Kim who would hand out assignments to the police staff, including the interviews with the other residents of Agate House.

She and Jake had discussed how to handle Rogers. For tonight, they decided not to arrest him. Parking on the street outside Phoebe's apartment didn't rise to the level of crime. But Jake arranged to keep Rogers's home under surveillance. The idea of standard police procedure seemed to please him. The Astoria cops didn't often handle stakeouts.

When she mentioned finding the photo of Alan Quilling and Phoebe in a steamy embrace, Jake had been disappointed but hadn't dismissed her suspicions. Similar to their plan for Rogers, they decided not to confront Quilling immediately. Instead, they curtailed his forensic activities and arranged for him to be on paid leave-of-absence.

Leaving the shower, Skylar felt renewed and energized. She dressed in skinny jeans and a T-shirt with an oatmeal-colored cable-knit cardigan covering her holster. With her hair brushed and hanging loose past her shoulders, she appeared tidy enough for a meeting with Crawford and his old buddy, Jimi. After a glance in the mirror above the bathroom sink, she dabbed on blush and lipstick. Jake would also be downstairs, and she didn't want to be pasty-faced and tired-looking. It was barely ten o'clock. Plenty of time to make progress on the case.

She heard a knock. Through the closed door, Jake said, "It's me, Detective Armstrong."

So formal. She wondered if he was embarrassed about visiting the room of an unmarried federal officer after dark. When she opened the door and confronted the large man who filled the doorframe, she saw nothing self-conscious in his manner. His intense blue-eyed gaze slid from the top of her head and her unbound hair to her lipstick to her sweater and jeans. He gave an appreciative nod. "You clean up good."

"That doesn't make sense. I'm not cleaning *up*. I changed out of my suit, which means I'm dressing *down*."

"I like this better."

When he entered, she realized the clothes she'd discarded when she stripped were still strewn across the duvet where she tossed them. With a swoop of her arm, she gathered her jacket, blouse and silky underwear, flung the garments into the closet and snapped the door closed.

Nonchalantly, she flipped her hair out of her eyes. "What's on your mind?"

"Here's the update." His brazen grin told her that he'd seen the undies and noticed the lacy trim. "Chief Kim deployed and deputized every individual who's ever worked as an officer. She gave them 'profiles' to fill out when they talked to potential witnesses and/or suspects."

Skylar wasn't sure she liked the idea of half-trained cops conducting interviews. "I'm impressed by her ability to respond so fast. Tell me about these profiles."

"Nothing that requires analysis. It's a questionnaire. Name, address, phone number and how did you know Phoebe. Anything that stands out is highlighted for future follow-up."

"Then we can run them through the FBI criminal database. And verify alibis."

"So far, we haven't got much," he said. "The ex-boyfriends on Tabitha's list don't like Phoebe but none sound homicidal. The other residents of Agate House barely knew her. Two of McKenna's friends and the bartender confirmed his alibi."

"And the stakeout?"

"Officer Dub Wagner finished up at the crime scene and volunteered. Nothing has happened yet, but Chief Kim thinks Dub has got to be tired. She wants me to assign someone else to take his place in a couple of hours."

So far, so good. But she wanted to solve this case before the Shadowkeeper struck again. "What's going on with Crawford and Jimi Kim?"

"They're up to their eyebrows in data from twenty years ago. They've got boxes of files. Also, charts, maps and game plans. Though they claim to be keeping open minds, their investigation is rooted in the past."

Not a surprise. From the moment she saw her partner pull the battered old file for the Lightkeeper's Curse from his bottom desk drawer in the Portland office, she recognized his obsession with the serial killer he failed to apprehend twenty years ago. Crawford needed closure almost as much as the victims. His current theory posited that the Lightkeeper had come out of retirement with a new moniker. *Shadowkeeper.* Though unusual for serial killers to take a break once they started, it had happened before. "Are you familiar with the BTK murderer in Kansas?"

"I don't know much. BTK stands for bind, torture and kill."

"Correct." She suppressed a shudder. "He stopped killing and took a thirteen-year hiatus before he started up again."

Jake stroked the line of his jaw, drawing her attention to the interesting dimple on his clean-shaven chin. No stubble. Though still not wearing a uniform, he was well-groomed. "I've got a hunch that it's *not* the same guy. The Lightkeeper took orders from a high priestess and thought he was ridding the world of evil. The Shadowkeeper—as you pointed out—is a narcissist and doesn't give a damn about the rest of the world."

"You don't think we're wasting our time by following up on clues about Phoebe?"

"I don't," he said. "The Shadowkeeper targeted her for a reason."

"Too bad we don't know why." As she reached for the doorknob, her stomach growled. "I don't suppose we'll be lucky enough to find snacks downstairs."

"Oh, there's food. Chief Kim is here. One of the perks of working for a pregnant boss is the parade of munchies."

Before leaving her room, Skylar grabbed her briefcase packed with files, crime-scene photos and her handy-dandy laptop for taking notes. There hadn't been time to transcribe her interviews with McKenna and Rogers, but she'd downloaded the parts she'd recorded on her phone. The required paperwork would come later.

The carpeting on the wide landing had a seashell pattern that extended to the magnificent oak staircase. She descended and followed the sound of her partner's voice from down the hall on the first floor.

SSA Crawford sounded excited and energetic. Unusual for him. In addition to his rep for being as handsome as the next Golden Bachelor, he was known for being laid-back and cool.

Another voice joined his. This speaker had clear enunciation but talked a mile a minute.

She entered a large parlor with a mix of Victorian furniture and more practical styles. The main feature was a four-foot-tall freestanding antique mahogany helm wheel, fully appropriate for the captain of a sailing vessel. A long, rectangular table provided a space for meetings. At the closer end of the table, Chief Vivienne Kim presided over an array of hummus, pita chips, samosas filled with kimchi, deep-fried eggrolls, doughnuts, pickles and Girl Scout cookies. Skylar's grumbling stomach drew her toward the feast. "This looks wonderful."

"I had to skip dinner," the chief said, "and I can't do that when I'm eating for two."

Her grandpa, Jimi Kim, introduced himself with a vigorous handshake and an explanation. "I called my wife, and Nana insisted on feeding Viv and the rest of the crew. We have bottled water and juice to drink. No coffee. No booze."

"Much appreciated." Skylar took an immediate liking to Jimi, a wiry man with neatly trimmed black hair turning gray at the temples. A wispy goatee encircled his mouth. His gentle smile didn't show his teeth.

"Come," he said, gesturing to the table. "Eat."

"Not yet," said Crawford. The senior agent stood at the helm, appropriate for the captain of this venture. "We have a lot to explain."

Jimi waggled a finger in his direction. "Not on an empty stomach."

Skylar helped herself to a plateful of food, grabbed a water bottle and found a seat near the other end of the table where Crawford and Jimi had arranged three standing easels. One held a map with markings, another showed the results of their meetings with two former suspects, and the third was a whiteboard covered with Crawford's scrawl.

"We'll start with the map," he said while she ate. "I've marked the locations of the seven Lightkeeper murders with red X's. You can see there are no repeats."

She swallowed a savory bite from a samosa. "Are all the locations lighthouses?"

"There were two actual lighthouses," he said. "North Head on Cape Disappointment and Cape Meares, which was where Phoebe was found. He didn't use the other two lighthouses in the area. Another is near the one on Cape Disappointment. Then, there's Terrible Tilly."

"Tell me about Tilly."

"It's on a one-acre basalt island about a mile offshore from where the Tillamook River merges with the Pacific. Iconic and impractical, the tower is battered by fierce winds and high surf that crashes as high as the beacon. Lightkeepers have died at that place. It was decommissioned as a lighthouse many years ago. Once it was used as a columbarium, but no more. Actually, I think it's for sale."

"Not my dream home," she said, scooping hummus onto a pita. "What about the other one on Cape Disappointment?"

"It's more difficult to get to. These other X's are for a light boat used by the coast guard, a miniature golf lighthouse, a motel and two restaurants with lighthouse themes."

The red marks on the map covered an area along several miles of coastal property, ranging from the Washington side of the Columbia River to Cannon Beach. Most of the murders had been in the vicinity of Astoria or Warrenton.

Skylar paused in her feeding frenzy to ask, "What's your takeaway on the map?"

"If the Shadowkeeper kills again, he might use one of these locations. Establishing physical surveillance on all of them is nearly impossible."

"I thought you arranged with FBI forensics team to set up virtual surveillance at all the possible sites."

"First thing tomorrow morning," SSA Crawford said. "We'll arrange for them to place cameras that feed into a closed-circuit system at APD headquarters, but this is a wide territory. We can't post enough trained officers to respond quickly."

"We have to try," Chief Kim said. "The cameras will provide more surveillance than guards at each place."

"It's a start." Jimi crossed the room and stood beside Crawford. "I may be an old man, but I am all in favor of modern technology. Things have changed for the better."

Crawford nudged his arm. "Think of what we could have done twenty years ago with the current improvements in DNA analysis and computer info in CODIS."

"Nowadays, crimes nearly solve themselves," Jimi said.

His granddaughter nibbled on a doughnut with rainbow sprinkles. "Are you admitting that the good old days weren't really so good?"

"Change is good. The Buddha says nothing is permanent, except change."

Skylar glanced toward Jake who was talking on his phone. When he pushed away from the table and left the room, she turned back to Crawford. "What else can we do?"

"I'm not totally convinced that the Shadowkeeper and the Lightkeeper are the same person. However, the Shadowkeeper has chosen to follow the patterns of the earlier murders." He pointed to the middle whiteboard. "The first heading: Warnings and Clues. The Lightkeeper left notes or sent messages that hinted at his next victim or the next location."

Not the first time SSA Crawford had mentioned these clues from the past. In his files, he'd copied these sometimes taunting and sometimes haunting comments.

Skylar asked, "Have we uncovered any other communication from the Shadowkeeper about his next victim? Or his next location? The cybercrime techies in Portland are usually able to track email addresses and give us a name. Surely they've come up with something."

"They haven't unraveled the computer routings." Crawford twisted the mahogany helm as though changing course. "That doesn't fit the pattern."

She asked, "How so?"

"The Shadowkeeper is clever enough to outwit the FBI's highly trained, sophisticated computer experts. That's very unlike the Lightkeeper. Twenty years ago, he made his audio recordings on cassettes, which was an outdated technology even then."

"A different profile." Though she believed they were dealing with two different killers, she also thought they'd learn something from the past. She stole a quick glance at the notes Crawford and Jimi had made about the two former suspects.

Before she could comment, Jake came back into the room and spoke for a moment with the chief who nodded her agreement. Swiftly, he approached Skylar and said, "Dub Wagner needs backup on his stakeout. Jolly Rogers is on the move."

Crawford shooed her toward the exit. "Go."

Chapter Twelve

Jake respected the investigative wisdom of SSA Crawford and former police chief Jimi Kim. Between them, the two lawmen had nearly fifty years' experience, and they were brilliant when it came to evaluating and reexamining the Lightkeeper evidence. More than expertise, they shared a fierce dedication. This was probably their last chance to revisit the serial murders from twenty years ago and finally nab the killer.

The procedure Jake and Skylar pursued was more simple and straightforward. *Who killed Phoebe Conway and why?* He was happy to leave the theoretical meeting behind and get back to basic police work.

Outside the Captain's Cove, he dashed down the stairs from the veranda to the street. Looking over his shoulder, he saw Skylar following. She paused on the sidewalk by his Explorer. With an eggroll in one hand and cookies in the other, she somehow managed to open the passenger door and climb inside. Breathless, she asked, "What's the problem with the stakeout?"

"The suspect is on the move, and Dub isn't sure what to do. Apart from Quilling, he's the youngest officer on the force. This is his first stakeout." Jake switched his phone to hands-free. "I have to call him to communicate. He didn't take his police car. So, no radio."

"That was smart procedure," she said. "Rogers would have noticed a cop car."

"So far, it seems like Dub has done everything right. He told me that he found a great place to park for surveillance. Far enough away to not arouse suspicion. Close enough to see if Rogers left."

"And then he did."

He nodded. "And Dub panicked. He's afraid he can't tail Rogers without being noticed, and he doesn't want to screw up."

Listening through earbuds, Jake followed Wagner's directions. To Skylar, he reported, "Rogers stopped at Billy's 24-Hour Trading Post where he apparently bought a pack of Marlboro cigarettes. As soon as he was outside, he lit up."

"Maybe that's why he left his house." She swallowed the last bite of eggroll. "Is he a regular smoker?"

"He quit several years ago."

"We must have stressed him out."

They were almost in sight of the Trading Post when Wagner gave new directions. Not wanting Rogers to see his Explorer with the Astoria Police logo, Jake pulled over to the curb. "Sounds like he's headed toward Highway 101."

She used a paper napkin with Halloween designs to dab at her lips. "This is the best meal I've had in quite a while. Nana Kim is a great cook."

And Skylar was a great eater—the kind of woman who enjoyed and appreciated food. When she'd changed out of her FBI suit into jeans, her personality had changed. Her features relaxed. She seemed more approachable. Her glossy auburn hair tumbled around her shoulders. He'd never seen anybody chow down with so much gusto, which made him eager to find out about her other appetites. "I'll let Nana Kim know you approve."

"Why the Girl Scout cookies?"

"The chief's oldest daughter is a Brownie and gets a prize for selling the most boxes."

"I should have guessed." She craned her neck and peered through the windshield at the swirling mists of fog. "We drove on Highway 101 to Cape Meares. Rogers could be going back there."

He never understood why criminals returned to the scene of the crime. Guilt. Pride. Fear that they'd left a clue. Didn't make logical sense, and Rogers wasn't that stupid. "We're not going to the highway. Rogers turned onto a side road and is driving to the west marina. We'll meet Dub there."

Jake took familiar shortcuts. He'd never owned a boat but had friends who did and knew his way around the piers, docks and marinas. Growing up in a harbor town, he'd spent a lot of time on the water and still enjoyed lazy afternoons, fishing on the river. He bypassed the turnoff to the Astoria-Megler Bridge and drove to a parking area on a hill above the marina where he easily located Officer Wagner's silver Subaru station wagon. Dub stood beside his front fender with a pair of binoculars raised to his eyes.

Jake greeted him with a compliment. "I thought you might be too tired to handle the stakeout after spending most of the day at the crime scene, but you're doing good."

"And I can use the overtime." He nodded to Skylar. "My wife is pregnant with our first. All the baby stuff costs a bundle."

"Congratulations." She pointed toward the marina. "Is the suspect alone?"

"I didn't see anybody in the car with him."

"May I use your binoculars? Nikon?"

"Yes, ma'am." He handed them over. "I've been itching to try these out, wondering if I should get infrared like the scope on my hunting rifle."

In this marina—one of several along the waterfront—

boats of varying size, shape and horsepower parked in the slips at either side of several interlocking docks.

She asked, "What's that little hut in the middle, the one with the light through the windows?"

"The harbormaster's shack. He's not usually available this late on a weeknight, but it looks like he's there."

"I wonder if he has surveillance cameras focused on the marina." She turned to Jake and passed the binoculars to him. "I spotted Rogers's trawler. The *Jolly Rogers*. Gotta be the one with the skull-and-crossbones flag."

He saw it immediately. In addition to streetlights along the dock, the small, enclosed cabin of Rogers's boat poured light onto the deck. "I'm not sure whether we should continue our stakeout from a distance or confront him directly."

"If we approach," she said, "he'll know we're suspicious."

"You already made that clear at the *Sun*. When he didn't have an alibi."

She appeared to be taken aback. "I didn't accuse him or arrest him."

"You've got that fed attitude that says don't-mess-with-me. You can be intimidating."

"Said the six-and-a-half-foot former marine," she scoffed.

"No such animal," he said. "Once a marine, always a marine."

"Got it."

"And I want to know why he came to the marina." Though the evidence against Rogers seemed to keep piling up, he couldn't bring himself to believe the newspaper man was guilty of stalking his employee and brutally murdering her. "If we don't question him, there's not much chance we'll find out what he's doing. We don't have enough evidence for a search warrant."

"Not nearly," she said, "and we need to be careful about

exerting undue pressure on a member of the press who can make us look bad."

His thinking took a different direction. "What if he's preparing his boat to make an escape? Remember how he talked about retirement and cruising up and down the coast?"

Skylar met his gaze, and he saw determination in her sea-green eyes as she came to a decision. "You're right. We can't stand here watching while he heads off into parts unknown."

He returned the binoculars to their owner. "Dub, I want you to stay here and keep an eye on Rogers. If he leaves, follow his car and continue your stakeout."

"Yes, sir."

Together, he and Skylar walked down to the marina, unlatched the gate and walked side by side on a long wooden pier. A narrow branch led them to the slip where the *Jolly Rogers* was docked. The trawler, with a black hull and white cabin, showed signs of its nearly twenty-year age as they got closer. Though Jake couldn't imagine shooting a man he'd known since he was a kid, he pushed aside his jacket for easy access to the Beretta in his holster. He noticed that Skylar had left her FBI windbreaker open. He saw the outline of her Glock and recalled her quick draw when facing Ty McKenna. He hoped she wouldn't need that skill.

"Something about this is all wrong."

"You're the one who wanted to approach the suspect," Skylar said.

"But Mr. Rogers?" In the back of his mind, the lyrics to "It's a Beautiful Day in the Neighborhood" played. "Mr. Rogers?"

Jake went first on the narrow dock beside the trawler. As soon as he and Skylar stood where the boat was moored, Rogers stuck his head out of the cabin and yelled, "What the hell are you doing here?"

Skylar didn't draw her weapon, but her head-on confrontation showed solid FBI aggressiveness. She was calling the shots, as she usually did. "Step out of the cabin and onto the deck," she snapped. "Show me your hands."

"Damn it, Armstrong," Rogers appealed to him. "What's her problem?"

"You'd better do what Special Agent Gambel says." *Always back up your partner.* "Our investigation has turned up evidence we need to ask you about."

"It's past my bedtime," Rogers complained. "Too damn late to play stupid games."

"Out on deck," Skylar repeated. "Now."

Instead of obeying her order, he hesitated, stuck an unlit cigarette between his lips and glared. "What are you going to do? Arrest me?"

Her voice went low and dangerous. "You asked for it, Rogers."

Before she could whip out her Glock, and before the newspaperman could toss out another dumb unedited comment, Jake climbed aboard the *Jolly Rogers*. After taking a moment to get his balance, he stood equidistant between the two adversaries.

"Hey!" The old man emerged from the cabin, stepped onto the deck and waved his hands in the air. Instead of his usual attire of a shirt and necktie with a loose knot, he wore an overlarge black hoodie that flapped around his arms like bat wings. "I damn well didn't give you permission to come aboard."

Without preface or explanation, Jake asked, "How often, in the past couple of weeks, was your vehicle parked near Phoebe's apartment house?"

"Why the hell would my car be there?"

"We have a witness who saw your black sedan with the skull-and-crossbones decal."

"They're lying," Rogers said. "It's his or her word against mine."

"A credible witness." Jake made direct eye contact. "Consider carefully before you speak. Was your car parked outside Agate House where Phoebe lived?"

Rogers reached into the pocket of his sweatshirt and took a Zippo lighter. The wind through the marina made it difficult to light his Marlboro, and he took his time. An effective ploy to irritate both Jake and Skylar. When he had a glow at the tip, Rogers said, "I was there. I had to talk to her about an assignment for the paper."

When Skylar stepped onto the deck beside him, Jake noticed—thankfully—that her Glock stayed in the holster. She asked, "What was your relationship with Phoebe?"

"None of your business," he said defiantly.

Jake cringed inside, not wanting to think of Rogers chasing Phoebe. Not that there was anything wrong with an older man dating a younger woman. The small town of Astoria couldn't claim to be immune to the cliché of an employee sleeping his or her way to the top. And the ick factor was nothing compared to cold-blooded murder. He prompted, "You were her boss."

"Goes without saying. She was my employee and a damn good reporter. Her articles on *The Goonies* upped our circulation."

"How many times did you visit her?" Skylar asked.

"I don't know. Maybe twice."

"Our witness saw your vehicle several times, enough that it attracted his attention."

"So what?" His thick eyebrows lowered in a scowl. "It's not illegal to park on the street. Did you think of that? Maybe I just happened to be in her area."

Skylar scowled. "I don't believe in coincidence."

"Lawyer," he shouted.

"One more question." Jake wanted to get as much info as possible. "Why did you come to the marina tonight?"

He inhaled deeply and blew his cigarette smoke into the fog. "I was looking for somebody and thought they might be here. But they aren't."

Trying to find a person who wasn't there? That excuse was just weird enough to be true. "Who?"

"I want my damn lawyer. You can't ask me any more questions."

Jake pushed again. "This person isn't here. Why can't you tell us about him or her?"

"Her," Rogers snapped. "It's a *her.*"

"Tell me about her. Hypothetically."

"She might be my alibi for the night when Phoebe was killed. Maybe I wasn't alone in bed. Maybe I won't give you her name because she's married to somebody else." He straightened his shoulders. "That's all I'm going to say. Now, get your sorry ass off my boat."

"While we're here," Jake said, "we could do a quick search."

"Don't push your luck, Armstrong. You're trespassing on my boat, and you have no right to be here unless you have a warrant."

"We have what we came for." Skylar climbed off the deck onto the pier. "Don't leave town, Mr. Rogers, not without telling me."

Jake followed her without a backward glance at the newspaper man. On the pier, he walked beside her. "What did you mean when you said we had what we came for?"

"He gave us an alibi for the time Phoebe was killed, which I suspect we can verify through the local gossip you're privy to. And he claimed his car had a work-related reason to be in Phoebe's neighborhood."

"Right."

"I don't believe either of those statements," she said, "but that's what we wanted to know."

Jake agreed with everything she said, especially about local gossip. If he put out a couple of feelers, he'd have the name, address and occupation of Rogers's lover in no time flat. The reason for visiting Phoebe presented more of a problem. "He's not telling the whole truth."

"I don't think he's the Shadowkeeper," she said.

"I agree."

"But I was right about him," she said. "The man definitely has something to hide."

Chapter Thirteen

Just past dawn the next morning—a few minutes after seven—Skylar stood at the street corner outside the Astoria Police Department. She hadn't gone to sleep last night until after two in the morning when she'd concluded her update for SSA Crawford and Jimi, filed the required reports, requested search warrants for Rogers's property and launched plans for this morning.

Those plans had been blown to hell. One untraceable text message on her phone shattered their investigation.

Hello Agent Skylar. The princess is in the tower. Such a pretty girl, she looks a bit like you, my dear. She wasn't a Disappointment. At the North Head Lighthouse. Phoebe would have written a full column about this little songbird and her silence. —The Shadowkeeper

The repeated ping from the text had wakened her less than an hour ago. The clues were blatant. Cape Disappointment. North Head Lighthouse.

Skylar bolted from the bed, notified Crawford and Jake, who said he'd contact Chief Kim. The chief would follow up on the message and try to track the phone that had placed the text. Confirmation of the text message came through before Skylar was fully dressed in her standard FBI outfit: gray suit, cotton shirt and black leather belt holster. On top, she wore a rain jacket, standard clothing for damp, foggy Astoria.

The chief had notified the Washington State Parks service, who established a crime scene and sent photos of a dark-haired woman hanging by her neck from the high lighthouse tower below the beacon while fog swirled around her body and night began to lift. Further investigation would wait until members of the task force in Astoria arrived. No identification had been made.

An hour earlier, she and Crawford had driven to the Astoria Police Department. He dropped her off to check in with Chief Kim while he drove to the crime scene. In the predawn, every light had been lit at the APD and every parking space filled. Officers—some in uniforms and some in plainclothes—had been working the phones from their desks or dashing through the corridors, seeking more information.

The investigation was in full swing. But they were too late. The Shadowkeeper had already struck again.

In the conference room, Chief Kim had offered doughnuts and coffee while she brought Skylar and Jake up to speed on other aspects of the investigation. Rogers's house had been under surveillance all night. After his trip to the marina, the suspect hadn't gone anywhere else.

Arrangements had been made with the FBI forensic and surveillance teams to set up cameras at likely spots for the Shadowkeeper to strike, which included the seven red *X*'s on the map that marked lighthouses and lighthouse replicas. One less now. The North Head Lighthouse.

Though hungry, Skylar had only nibbled the edge of a plain doughnut and sipped a mild tea. No coffee. Not yet. She needed to pamper her stomach in case of potential queasiness. Today, she had her own secret trial. Her own phobia.

On the street corner in Astoria, she slowly lifted her chin, turned northwest and confronted the monster that stood between her and the crime scene.

Today, Skylar would cross that bridge.

Random facts blasted through her mind, providing zero consolation. The Astoria-Megler Bridge over the Columbia River was over four miles, the longest cantilevered truss bridge in the country. *Anybody would be scared, right?* Clearance above the water was over two hundred feet—high enough for container ships and Carnival cruise vessels to pass through on their way to Portland. The trusses and towering framework resembling the backbone of a T. rex hunched over the two-lane traffic.

Clear skies this morning showed the monster in all its glory. She inhaled through her nose and exhaled in a whoosh through her mouth. Over the years, she'd learned that meditation also soothed, but there wasn't time to drop into a mindful session. Taking a sedative was out of the question. She had to be alert while working the crime scene.

She'd make it across the damn bridge. She had to.

Jake hiked toward her on the sidewalk with long, fast strides. Occasionally, he glanced over his shoulder as if he were being chased. Errant rays of sunshine glistened in his blond hair. He looked angry. He stalked toward his Explorer in the parking lot, and she fell into step beside him. Trying to match her stride with his very long legs, she was almost jogging.

Before they reached his vehicle, the threat he'd been avoiding on the sidewalk caught up to them. Three young women, aggressively snapping photos of Jake with their phones, surrounded them and shouted questions about the investigation. They represented Astoria's media coverage. Blond. Bright-eyed. Enthusiastic.

"No comment," Jake said coldly.

"Somebody else got murdered, huh?"

"Who is it? Come on, Detective Armstrong, tell us. My

older sister, Juliet, didn't come home last night. She's blond like Phoebe. Is it her?"

Skylar silently vetoed Juliet. The Shadowkeeper said that the victim looked like her, which meant dark or auburn hair color. But she knew better than to say anything to the press. One response would lead to another to another.

Undeterred, the trio trailed behind them.

At Jake's car, another individual appeared. She was tall and solid. When she moved, her scarves swirled, and her bangle bracelets jingled. Dagmar. Jake's cousin and the daughter of the Lightkeeper's final victim. Dagmar, the alibi for Pyro Pierce.

In most instances, Skylar would have been annoyed at further interference, but she approved when Dagmar snarled at the blondies and told them to bug off. The ladies of the press took a step back while she and Jake entered the SUV. Before they could stop her, Dagmar leaped into the back.

Skylar snapped. "We can't give you a ride."

"I'll be gone in a minute," Dagmar said. "I have info."

Driving carefully to avoid crashing into one of the reporter/blogger/influencer gang, Jake merged into Astoria's meager imitation of the seven-to-nine rush hour. Instead of thanking his cousin, he threw out an accusation. "You're dating my old science teacher, Pyro Pierce."

"Have you got a problem with that?"

"The opposite. He's a great guy."

"Stop calling him Pyro. He's only had six major explosions in the chem lab. And I think he's cute without eyebrows." She shifted in the back seat. "Anyway, I have information for you. About Joe Rogers's gal pal."

Skylar swiveled her head so she could see Dagmar. "How did you hear about that? We only found out last night."

"I'm a librarian." Dagmar shrugged. "I know things."

"Her name?" Jake asked.

"Delilah Miller. She runs a beauty salon."

Skylar took a moment to digest the fact that Delilah—the Biblical seductress known for cutting Samson's hair—ran a salon. Astoria had to be the quirkiest place she'd ever worked. "This Delilah. Is she married?"

"Separated," Dagmar said. "Attractive. Curvy. Has magenta hair. Surprisingly age-appropriate for Rogers. They've been dating for over a year. If you ask me, she's using the 'married' excuse to avoid getting too close to Jolly Rogers."

"Or vice versa," Skylar said.

"Drop me off at Toast-To-Go," Dagmar said. "Don't suppose you'll tell me the name of the victim."

Jake scoffed. "Listen, Dagmar, you've got to back off. Let us do our job."

"Sure thing, cuz. Let the cops handle it? Sure, that worked really well twenty years ago."

He pulled up outside the corner coffee shop, let his cousin out and watched her enter. "I sure as hell hope she doesn't get herself into trouble. Dagmar looks fierce, but—in some ways—she's fragile."

Oddly enough, Skylar could identify. Like Dagmar, she cultivated a tough exterior. "Her mother's murder must have been devastating."

"When her mom died, her father didn't want to be saddled with a kid. He took off. She had no family, except for my dad and me." Remembering, he frowned and stroked his clean-shaven chin. "Probably wasn't the best thing for Dagmar to be raised by a high school football coach. There was nobody in her life to add a feminine touch."

"I grew up with two brothers." Her mother had always participated in her life, but Mom was a judge, not exactly someone who encouraged her to collect dolls. Though she and Jake had been together almost nonstop since she arrived in Astoria, they really hadn't talked much about their families or hobbies or private life. If she knew him better, she might have mentioned her phobia. Or not...probably not. "Did you play football?"

"When I was seventeen, I was my full height. Six feet, six inches. And my dad was the coach. So, yeah, I played. Wasn't very good. Kept tripping over my own big feet. Dad said it'd take a while for me to grow into my body. When I did, I joined the marines. *Semper fi.*"

Before Skylar had a chance to prepare herself for what was to come, he swerved onto the circular approach to the Highway 101 bridge. The curve gradually climbed to the full elevation above the wide Columbia. She looked down at treetops and houses as they ascended higher and higher. Acrophobia wasn't her problem. She didn't love heights but could handle them. It was bridges...always bridges. *Gephyrophobia.*

Eyes open. Eyes closed. Her pulse accelerated to a staccato drumbeat. Quietly, she hummed the lyrics. "Left a good job in the city..." Her blood surged. A high-pitched squeal overwhelmed "Proud Mary" and echoed against her eardrums.

Eyes open, her gaze darted across the clear blue sky, seeking an escape from the torturous noise. A terrible whine. It thinned and faded but didn't go silent. The high note competed with the rumble of tires on pavement.

She trembled, knotted her fingers together to keep from showing her lack of control. Her gaze flicked downward, and she was struck with paralyzing vertigo. The inside of her head whirled fast and faster on a whirling carousel.

Eyes closed, closed, closed. She barely constrained her nausea. A sour taste crawled up the back of her throat.

She heard Jake speaking. "Are you okay, Skylar?"

"Fine. I'm fine."

Her eyes stayed closed. She felt rather than saw their descent to a level closer to the water, but there were still miles to go before they reached the Washington side. Fireworks went off inside her head. With each explosion, pop and sizzle, the pressure increased. A vice grip encircled her head and squeezed from either side. Tighter and tighter. One more turn of the screw, and her skull would be crushed.

She heard Jake calling to her. "Skylar, open your eyes. Look at me. You're not okay."

"Fine."

"I can't stop here. I have to keep moving until we're off the bridge."

"Don't stop."

Behind her closed eyes, she saw the darkest shade of black. Ebony. Not a trace of light.

She couldn't breathe. Couldn't move. Falling, overwhelmed by inky blackness. *Losing control.* She plunged headfirst into unconsciousness.

TIME LOST ALL form and meaning. She felt like only a minute had lapsed, but she might have been knocked out for hours. Still seated in the Explorer, the upholstered seat supported her back. Her feet rested on the floor mat. She heard the passenger door open, felt the latch on her seat belt snap.

Strong arms wrapped around her, and he pulled her out of the car. A fresh breeze caressed her cheek. Half awake, standing, she leaned against the front fender. Her eyelids fluttered open. She saw Jake.

"W-where are we?" she stammered.

"On the Washington side of the bridge. I parked on the shoulder." Gently, he held her upper arms and supported her so she wouldn't collapse onto the pavement. "No matter how many times you tell me you're fine, I don't believe you. Something happened on the bridge."

"Yes." She couldn't explain. If she admitted to having a debilitating phobia, she worried she'd lose her job as a special agent and be assigned to a desk. "But it's over."

He didn't argue with her or demand that she come clean. Instead, he offered warmth and a comforting embrace. She rested her cheek against his chest. The big, brawny marine held her with the softest touch imaginable.

For a moment, she snuggled into the folds of his merino wool vest and inhaled his clean scent. Cedarwood and pine. He smelled like a forest at sunrise when the dew had evaporated. She could have stayed there for hours.

But the lighthouse and the crime scene were on the road ahead. There was work to be done.

"We should get going," she said.

"You were singing 'Proud Mary.' Why?"

"I'm a big Tina Turner fan."

"Me, too."

With her head tilted back, she gazed past the dimple on his chin to his mouth. "I'm really okay. It must have been something I ate. A mild case of food poisoning."

"Yeah, sure."

"Sometimes, I get really tired." She wanted to talk about her phobia but wouldn't. Not yet. "There's no rational explanation for why I passed out."

"It's okay. You don't have to tell me."

"I'm not afraid."

"I didn't say you were." He leaned closer. Close enough to kiss. Close enough that she felt the warmth of his breath on her forehead. "You're a trained federal agent, Skylar. A brown belt in karate. A trained markswoman. You have all the tools to take care of yourself."

But how could she do battle with a bridge? She peered into the depths of his dark blue eyes. "It's irrational. The closest I can come to explaining is that I'm overwhelmed by a sense of vulnerability."

"Nothing wrong with that," Jake said. "Vulnerable is another word for sensitive. Sympathetic. You're open."

A one-word explanation. One syllable. "Weak."

"Never," he said.

She wanted desperately to believe he was right.

Chapter Fourteen

Tucked back into the passenger seat of the Explorer, Skylar concentrated on regulating her breathing and centering her thoughts. After a few miles on Highway 101 following the course of the Columbia and heading toward Cape Disappointment, she felt more in control and had stopped shivering.

On the way back to normal, she was hungry again and wished for a venti-size French roast. Her meltdown on the monster bridge had been one of the most extreme phobic reactions she'd ever had, possibly due to the stress of the investigation. It was a relief that she'd been with Jake instead of SSA Crawford.

If she'd been riding with her supervisor, there would have been consequences. Though Crawford respected her level of experience and gave her a lot of leeway, she was still on probationary status as a special agent in a field investigation. Hyperventilating and fainting were most definitely not acceptable behaviors. Sometime soon, she'd need to give Jake a better explanation than food poisoning or lack of sleep. The truth. She'd have to tell him the truth.

That surprising conclusion caused her to gasp. A shudder rattled down her spine, and her fingers twitched as if losing her grasp. Though she'd had gephyrophobia for as long as she could remember, she'd never told anyone. Not her parents or her brothers or her best friends. She never wanted to be seen as a person who had problems she couldn't handle. Even her name stood for strength. Skylar was mighty, a warrior in battle and a leader in peace. Yet, she found herself seriously thinking about confiding in Jake, a man she'd known for only a day.

In his calm, conversational baritone, Jake said, "If we'd turned right instead of left when we got off the bridge, we'd be headed to Dismal Nitch."

The area around Astoria contained a boatload of weird history, some of which she was beginning to actually enjoy. "I'm sure there's a story behind that name."

"Lewis and Clark had almost reached the Pacific, the end of the trail, when their expedition was stopped from further progress by wind, rain and—you guessed it—fog. They hunkered down near the river. Starving and soaked to the skin, they were miserable. In his journal, Clark referred to the campsite as Dismal Nitch. Little did he know, they were only a couple of miles away from the ocean."

"I guess that proves what you said earlier." She smiled. "The Pacific Northwest ain't for sissies."

"Guess so."

When he shot her a glance, his gaze showed concern. He must be questioning her breakdown, but he didn't make verbal accusations or ask if she was okay. Instead, he seemed willing to accept her panic attack and move forward, which was fine with her. *No muss, no fuss, don't look at us.* "How far are we from the lighthouse?" she asked.

"Half an hour or so. Your partner is already at the scene, right?"

"You bet he is." SSA Crawford had been anxious. He told her that he hoped Phoebe's murder hadn't been a harbinger of other deaths. The discovery of a second victim meant this crime should be investigated as the beginning of serial killings—part of the Lightkeeper's Curse. "I'm guessing he picked up former Chief Kim on the way."

"Smart move. Everybody in this part of the world knows and loves Jimi Kim."

"And his wife's cooking."

"I'm guessing that you're hungry again," he said. "No problem. We'll stop in Ilwaco and pick up coffee and a bite."

Though she felt guilty about not rushing directly to the scene, she really needed a boost of caffeine and calories to charge her system.

Being slow to report for duty didn't compare to the regret she felt about not preventing the second murder. She and Crawford had literally been in the vicinity when the Shadowkeeper killed again. She should have stressed the urgency for the FBI forensics teams to set up their surveillance. They hadn't baited the trap. She exhaled a sigh. "You know, if we'd had the cameras in place, we might have caught a glimpse of the killer."

"We might have a sighting, anyway. Chief Kim assigned a team to review footage from the traffic cams on the bridge."

"I never thought of that," she admitted. The damn bridge might be useful, after all.

They stopped at a roadside convenience store and gas station to grab coffee and packaged burritos that were surprisingly tasty after being heated in a microwave. In minutes, her energy and confidence returned. She was back to the investigation with her faculties fully intact. No time for second-guessing. She had to find the Shadowkeeper wherever he was lurking.

While Jake drove through a thickly forested wildlife preserve, he devoured his burrito. "I can't help but wonder… Why did the Shadowkeeper send that text to your phone? How did he get the number?"

"Chief Kim said the caller's phone was untraceable. My contact numbers are no secret. I often write them on business cards I hand out to witnesses."

"He said the victim looked like you. How would he know unless he's stalking you?"

"Everybody knows everything in Astoria," she reminded him.

"There could be deeper reasons."

"The behavioral analysis people would probably draw all sorts of psychological inferences from the text, but I think it's something less complex. The Shadowkeeper is childish, as many narcissists are, and he's teasing us."

"That's what Rogers said when he read the message that mentioned me."

"His messages have been snarky," she said. "And he's playing a game. Giving us a series of clues to prove he's smarter than we are."

When Jake turned into the parking lot for the North Head Lighthouse, he had to show his badge to a Washington officer who monitored the entrance and advised people that this area had been designated as a crime scene. Similar to Cape Meares, law enforcement from many jurisdictions had responded. Skylar thanked her lucky stars that she wasn't the special agent in charge of this chaos. SSA Crawford won that prize.

Instead of leaping from the Explorer, Jake parked and turned toward her. "Let's see what we can figure out."

"Okay."

"In addition to the location, the main point in his text seems to be about the songbird. Not sure what that means."

"When we have a victim identification, we'll know more."

He studied her with a bit of concern. "Are you good to go?"

"Ready as I'll ever be."

They left the Explorer and walked side by side down a curving asphalt path through a forest of pine, cedar, scarlet maple, golden aspen and hemlock. There was a chill in the October air. Fog dimmed the morning sunrise, and the wind hummed through the branches and boughs in a haunting melody interrupted by the cries of gulls and terns. In a clearing to their right, she saw a couple of two-story residences offering overnight lodging for tourists. Smoke spiraled from the chimneys, adding the scent of burnt firewood to the salty ocean air.

When they came out of the forest and stepped onto the rocky promontory above the Pacific, they saw the whitewashed lighthouse tower, sixty-five feet tall. Similar to the setup at Cape Meares, a small house adjoined the tower. The automated beacon continued to flash, two bursts of light every thirty seconds.

She caught her breath. "This is way more impressive than the other one."

"The tower had to be taller," Jake said, "because the cliff isn't as high."

From the crime-scene photos she'd received, Skylar knew what to expect and wasn't looking forward to viewing the body. From where they stood, she and Jake couldn't see the woman dangling at the end of a noose. The forensic investigators wearing gloves and Tyvek booties had congregated on the seaward side of the tower. Several markers on the ground indicated evidence that might help solve the case.

She straightened her posture and went forward on the path that encircled the lighthouse. The victim gradually came into view.

She'd been hung by the neck from an iron gallery encircling the tower at the level of the beacon. Death by hanging made a horrific display, especially since the victim wore a skimpy outfit for this time of year—a sleeveless burgundy tank top and short, cutoff jeans. The heels of her red, pointed-toe cowboy boots clunked against the tower when the wind tossed her in one direction and another. The victim's wrists were cuffed in front. A bandanna blindfold covered the upper half of her face and a rectangle of silver masking tape had been slapped across her mouth. Except for her nose, her features could neither be seen nor identified. And yet her hair was pulled back and the bruising on her throat was visible.

Officer Dot Holman—in a pressed uniform with an APD jacket—joined them. Her elfin face wore a mask of sorrow. "I knew her. Lucille Dixon."

Surprised, Skylar asked, "How can you tell who she is?"

Without turning to confront the gruesome sight, Dot said, "I'd recognize those boots anywhere. Plus, she has a tattoo on her upper right arm. A yellow rose with a long stem that goes all the way to her elbow."

"As in 'The Yellow Rose of Texas,'" Jake said. "She always wore that kind of outfit with her trademark boots when she sang at the Sand Bar."

The name of the tavern sounded familiar. Then Skylar remembered. The Sand Bar was where Ty McKenna established his alibi with his drunk friends.

The connection between the victim and a suspect bore further examination. Or maybe not. So many people in this area knew each other that it would be strange if the victim, Lucille Dixon, didn't have friends in the inner circle of her investigation.

Both Dot and Jake were solemn. Lucille must have been someone worth knowing.

When Skylar looked up again, she saw a thin ray of sunlight gleaming off SSA Crawford's white hair. He stood at the railing above the noose and appeared to be studying the knot in a heavy-duty rope similar to those used in boating. Crawford looked down, saw her and gave a nod before entering a door into the lighthouse. While Jake stayed to talk with Dot, Skylar headed toward the entrance into the North Head Lighthouse where she waited for Crawford.

In minutes, he stepped through the door and approached her. "Glad you're here. We have a lot of ground to cover. And I want to move fast."

He didn't need to warn her that the killer might attack another woman tonight. Skylar was already counting down the hours until nightfall in her head. "I can help gather information here at the scene."

"Our FBI forensic team is already on the job," he said. "As soon as they arrived from Portland, I pulled them away from setting up surveillance cameras and told them to process the lighthouse. I'm sure they'll find prints and trace evidence, but this little house is a tourist site. Strangers are tromping in and out all day."

"We'll learn more from the ME," she said.

"Dr. Kinski and her people will be here soon to remove the body and transport her to the autopsy suite where she'll join Phoebe Conway."

Two for the price of one. She kept that irreverent comment to herself. "We have a tentative identification. Lucille Dixon, a singer at a local tavern. Her occupation syncs with the Shadow's mention of a songbird."

"I've heard her name."

"Do you have a theory about how the murder happened?"

"I always do." Seeking privacy, he directed her to the outer edge of the path and spoke in quiet tones that no one else could hear. "The Shadowkeeper either enticed the songbird to meet him here, or he brought her here in his own vehicle."

"You think she came willingly, like on a date."

"It's possible. The traffic cams on the bridge can give us more information. Once they were here, he needed to get her to the upper level using the winding staircase."

She thought of three possibilities. "He could have convinced her to make the climb herself. Or forced her to climb using a gun or some other weapon. Or he might have drugged her and carried her up the staircase."

Crawford nodded. "Dr. Kinski will run a tox screen for drugs and can tell us if cause of death was strangulation by hanging or being choked with his hands."

She nodded. "The forensic team might be able to determine where she was strangled. From prints, fibers and scuff marks at Cape Meares, they suspect Phoebe was unconscious, then strangled and finally posed on the staircase."

"Could be what happened here," Crawford said. "If she was convinced to meet him on her own—like a date—I'd think the Shadowkeeper was a younger man."

"You know better than that," she said with a grin. Crawford wasn't called the Silver Fox for nothing. "Plenty of young women are attracted to older men."

"I didn't say that Jimi and I were giving up on proving that the Shadowkeeper and the Lightkeeper are one and the same. Which reminds me…" He raised an eyebrow. "Even with the stakeout at his house, are you certain Rogers didn't sneak out last night?"

"It's possible." The stakeout was being handled by inexperienced officers, and Rogers might be more clever than they gave him credit for. "This morning, we learned the name of the woman who was his supposed alibi for the night of Phoebe's murder."

"Follow up on that this morning. Then, you and Jake need to go to the Sand Bar and find out who Lucille was dating. Guys who were interested in her and so on. You know the drill."

"Yes, sir." She heard what he was saying, but her mind filled with images of the bridge, and her gut wrenched. She'd have to cross again.

He patted her shoulder. "I'll stay here at the scene. You and Jake have made significant inroads among the locals regarding Phoebe's murder. That's where I want you to focus."

"Yes, sir."

She had her marching orders. Though she would have liked to observe the forensics at the crime scene and avoid the bridge for as long as possible, she understood the need to gather information and talk to witnesses. They needed answers, needed to shine a spotlight on the Shadowkeeper before he killed another victim.

Chapter Fifteen

Outside the North Head Lighthouse, Jake watched two muscular guys in FBI T-shirts rig a pulley system on the wrought iron gallery wrapped around the upper level of lighthouse tower outside the beacon. They attached the pulley to the rope and severed the original rope below the knot. The railing where the rope had been tied was about fifty feet above the asphalt path. The noose around Lucille's throat hung down another ten feet, which meant her cowboy boots dangled thirty to thirty-five feet overhead. The discussion about whether to lower her body from inside or out had been fierce, but Dr. Kate Kinski prevailed. She convinced everybody, including Jake, that the interior option would cause more postmortem contusions and contamination of potential evidence. Hence, the pulley system.

The two husky FBI forensic techs—nobody had bulging pecs and biceps like those without regular bodybuilding workouts—removed the portion of rope that had been tied to the railing and bagged the knots as evidence for further forensic study. Slowly and carefully, they used the pulley to lower the victim to Kinski and her assistants from the ME's office, who stood below, waiting with a gurney. They all wore protective Tyvek suits and booties as well as nitrile gloves.

Since Kinski couldn't get close enough to study the bruise

pattern on the victim's throat, she refused to speculate on whether death came from manual strangulation or from hanging from the noose. Any supposition would be pure guesswork until the autopsy this afternoon, but Jake couldn't imagine the Shadowkeeper being dumb enough to drag a victim who was alert to the top of the interior staircase, much less fling her over the edge. Seemed logical that Lucille was already dead or unconscious when she was hanged.

Skylar peered down from the gallery, watching as the body descended inch by inch. Then she looked away, raised her head and gazed out to sea. A gust of wind brushed her auburn hair off her forehead, and she tucked a strand behind her ear. If they hadn't been investigating a murder, he wondered if she would have waved and called out to him. The unusually sunny day with a light breeze contrasted the aura of tragedy that hung over the grotesque crime scene.

A second victim. Though he didn't know her well, Jake would never forget Lucille Dixon. The songbird was a tiny woman who made a lot of noise. She had a big, raucous laugh and loved to dance the Texas two-step. Now she was gone. Brutally, senselessly murdered. Others would die...unless he and Skylar stopped the Shadowkeeper.

He watched the assistants in their Tyvek bunny suits maneuver the body onto the gurney while Dr. Kinski shouted instructions about how they shouldn't disturb the knots in the noose. Jake was too far away to get a clear look at her face. Not that he wanted to.

Looking up, he saw Skylar again. She pointed to her black titanium field watch, shook her head and shrugged. Probably meaning she wasn't quite ready to go. She seemed to have recovered from her earlier meltdown on the bridge.

Yeah, the bridge. He'd noticed the timing. Yesterday, she'd been struck by a similar tension when they crossed the less imposing bridge over Youngs Bay. He worried about when the next incident would occur. She sure as hell wasn't weak, but she had a flaw—an irrational reaction triggered by bridges. During his tours of duty in the marines, he'd seen similar attacks suffered by combat veterans. Overwhelming panic. A waking nightmare. PTSD.

He knew better than to suggest that she get a grip and ignore it. The nature of her disorder didn't make sense and couldn't be controlled. But he had an idea about how he might help her. He took out his phone and placed a call.

No sooner had he made the necessary arrangements and disconnected than his phone rang. Chief Vivienne Kim was calling with an update.

"A new email message just came through," she said. "It was sent to the *Astoria Sun* page for comments from readers. Hasn't been posted yet."

Not unexpected, but damn. He hated this. The killer wanted his chance to gloat, to let them know they were no match for him. "Does he say anything about the victim?"

"He does not."

"We have reason to believe it's Lucille Dixon."

"I know. Dot texted me." She sighed loudly. "I hate this."

Me, too. "Send the message to my cell phone and to Skylar's. Make sure Crawford and your grandpa have a copy."

"When you leave Cape Disappointment," she said, "you and SA Skylar are going to the autopsy, correct?"

"First, we need to check in with a potential witness at Delilah's Hair Salon and others at the Sand Bar where Lucille worked. Then the autopsy. But don't worry, I'll stay in touch."

He scrolled down his phone screen and read:

All the pretty princesses should form a club for the popular people. Ty McKenna would be invited. And you, Agent Skylar, would be their queen. A winner. A star. A hole-in-one. Too bad Phoebe isn't here to write about the true fate of beauty in her column. It never lasts for long.

He signed off as Shadowkeeper. Bitter and hostile.

Skylar stepped up beside him. She'd shed her rain jacket and adjusted her suit jacket to hide her holster. "I'm ready to go."

"Let's wait for these guys to move on." He pointed to the team of ME bunnies who were rattling along the asphalt path with the gurney. He handed her his phone. "I just got this from Chief Vivienne. It was emailed to the *Sun* reader comments page. They had the good sense not to post it."

She read and cursed under her breath. "Mentioning me, again. And McKenna."

"I'm beginning to think we let the hippest guy in town off the hook too soon."

"The hole-in-one reference seems obvious," she said. "And he also mentions a club. A golf club, perhaps. There's a lighthouse at a miniature golf course, right?"

"We'll go there if we have time. Our most important job today is the autopsy in Warrenton. On the other side of Youngs Bay. Across the bridge."

He watched her for a reaction. As she trekked up the pathway to the parking area, her shoulders stiffened, and she winced—an indication of her discomfort at the mention of a bridge.

"First, we go to Warrenton," she said, "although I have no idea why your county medical examiner is based there instead of Astoria. Warrenton is even smaller."

"The population is a little over six thousand," he said as he approached the Explorer and used his fob to unlock the doors. "The town marks the last campsite of the Lewis and Clark expedition and was home to Fort Stevens."

She fired a sharp glance in his direction. "How do you know all this stuff?"

"I worked as a tour guide in high school and then again when I got out of the marines."

"Really?" Her eyes narrowed as she absorbed this shred of trivia about his life. "I would have expected you to do something more…physical."

"Why? Because I'm extra large?" he scoffed. "Do they teach stereotyping in the FBI?"

"As something to avoid."

"You're a pretty woman," he said. "Does that mean you should be a model?"

"Okay, I got the point."

"I'm into learning stuff, like my cousin Dagmar. It's satisfying." She was about to discover the value of his tour guide experience. "There's something I want to talk to you about before we get back to town."

They settled into the Explorer and exited the parking area. He drove behind the ME's van back toward Astoria. Neither of them were using flashers or sirens to race through traffic. Not an emergency situation. Autopsies and interrogations accounted for their regular business on a Thursday morning.

He was about to explain his plan when her phone buzzed and she answered.

"It's Crawford," she whispered to him.

Her end of the conversation consisted mainly of "yessir" and "no sir." Clearly, she was getting her orders for the day. When she ended the call, she turned to him.

"You have new information," he said.

"They did an on-scene fingerprint analysis on the victim. Lucille Anne Dixon wasn't a saint. Her prints popped in AFIS. She has a criminal record."

He wasn't shocked. Lucille worked as singer in a tavern,

not in a nunnery. "Let me guess. Drunk and disorderly? Speeding tickets?"

"She was acquitted on felony theft charges when she apparently robbed an ex-boyfriend, and she was twice convicted of vandalism."

He shook his head. "I might have been the arresting officer on one of those vandalism charges. It had something to do with graffiti. Once again, an ex-boyfriend was involved."

"This doesn't give us a motive for why the Shadowkeeper went after her," Skylar said. "But Lucille had the habit of associating with dangerous people."

"Don't blame the victim," he said.

"I'm not. I'm just saying that she wasn't cautious."

"Like Garth Brooks said, she had 'Friends in Low Places.' Nothing wrong with that." He remembered watching Lucille perform. "She sang a lot of the country-western classics. Her sign-off was always the same. 'Your Cheatin' Heart.'"

"Could be a motive," she said. "We should pay close attention to her boyfriends."

He drove into Ilwaco behind the ME's ambulance van but turned onto a different route. There hadn't been time to explain his reasoning to her, but he believed he was doing the right thing. "We're taking a detour."

Suspicious, she asked, "Where are we going?"

"I'm asking you to trust me."

"The most dangerous words in the English language. Trust me."

"Hear me out." He parked outside the harbor where dozens of boats—all shapes and sizes—were docked. Exiting the Explorer, he came around to open her door.

When she stepped out and faced him, her hazel-green eyes held a million questions, and her full lips stretched in a stern, unbending line. Obviously, Skylar wasn't a woman who liked surprises. She growled. "We can't be wasting time. There's a lot to do."

"Right."

"You've got five minutes, Armstrong."

"Remember how I told you that I used to work as a tour guide? Well, here's another bit of trivia. From 1921 until 1966 when the Astoria-Megler Bridge opened, this stretch of the Columbia was regularly serviced by a three-ferry system. After the bridge was built, they sold the boats."

"Talk faster." She tapped her wristwatch. "Three minutes left."

"Nautical traffic in this part of the river is regulated," he said, calmly and slowly. Not to be rushed by her self-imposed deadline, he guided her toward the boats bobbing in the light waves. Circling gulls squawked a greeting while they walked. "The giant cargo ships and cruise vessels have to be guided through the bridge by port pilots. The man I worked for, Two-Toes Tucker, was a port pilot—"

"Wait! His name was Two-Toes?"

"Nickname. He lost two toes on his left foot in some kind of boating accident. He claims it was a shark attack. Anyway, he ran a sightseeing business—Tucker's Tug Tours—cruising from Astoria to the coast and along the Pacific from Ilwaco to Tillamook."

Her hostility began to thaw, and she looked away from her watch. "A tugboat?"

"Seaworthy and cute."

"I like tugs," she said. "A small boat with a powerful engine to move huge obstacles."

Like her. At the edge of a pier, he stepped aside and gestured toward the red-and-white boat trimmed with gold and emblazoned with the logo for Tug Tours. "Here's your ride across the Columbia. I told you she was cute."

"You shouldn't have gone to all this trouble."

But he could tell she was pleased. Her radiant smile made him want to go to even greater lengths. He'd swim the harbor with her on his back to keep her away from that damn bridge. When their gazes met, a lightning bolt crashed into the center of his chest and reverberated through his entire body. "It only took a phone call. Tucker was happy to help out. He knows my dad, and the two of them are conspiring to get me married and settled down. So, please ignore any of his attempts at matchmaking."

He felt like he'd said too much, but he couldn't help adding, "You don't have to tell me why you don't like bridges. I'm not judging or complaining. You're my partner, and I care about you."

With determined strides, she came closer to him. Less than a foot away, she rose up on her tiptoes and wrapped her arms around his neck. Her slender body molded to his. Her breasts crushed against his torso. Though he hadn't expected a reward like this, he adapted. Wrapping her in a firm embrace, he adjusted his position and intensified their contact.

Tentatively, her mouth joined with his, tasting his lips. He wanted a lot more from her. He hadn't expected this kind of spectacular contact when he arranged for her tugboat ride. Not on a conscious level. Of course, he'd been attracted to her from the first moment he saw her. But he never planned to put the moves on a fed.

She kissed like she meant it. Full contact. Full pressure. Nothing gentle about it. Her kiss held a whisper of desire, and he responded with a full-bodied roar of lust.

As suddenly as the kiss had started, they broke contact and separated. Breathing heavily, both of them stared at each other as if in a trance.

Then, she spoke. "Thank you, partner."

Chapter Sixteen

The midsize tugboat with a bright red hull and a white wheel-house painted with gold trim met Skylar's expectations for a friendly sightseeing ride. The roof of the wheelhouse had been modified for sunbathing, and the front deck had been expanded and enclosed by sturdy but decorative railings.

Standing at the bow, she waved goodbye to Jake who went ashore after he introduced her to the business owner, Two-Toes Tucker. She managed to maintain her poise, even though the incredible sensations unleashed when Jake kissed her still lingered on her lips. Her legs were still weak at the knees. Her pulse chugged more furiously than the powerful motor of the tugboat, which Tucker told her was capable of pulling eight tons or more.

"Jake's a good man," Tucker said. The white-haired gent with a full beard gave a signal to a salty redheaded woman who was visible through the window of the on-deck wheel-house, and the boat lurched forward. "That's my niece. I'm teaching her how to run the sightseeing biz. Wish I could get Jake to come back."

"He seems happy being a detective."

"How long have you been friends with him?"

"Not that long," she admitted. Tucker had probably seen their kiss and was sizing her up as a potential mate who would make Jake settle down. That opinion might be preferable to being labeled unprofessional.

"I don't rightly know much about you, young lady, but I'm guessing you're new in town. Are you here about the murders?"

"I'm with the FBI," she said. "You might know my partner, Supervisory Special Agent Harold Crawford."

"Damn right, I do. He's friends with Chief Jimi Kim."

She hadn't done much boating, and the sounds of the harbor played a maritime symphony in her head. The rhythmic lap of waves. The whistling winds. Cries from terns and gull. And the rumble of boat motors. When they cruised past a coast guard cutter, Tucker's niece tooted a spunky little foghorn and the guard responded.

Being on the water didn't bother Skylar, not like the bridges. But when the tug chugged under the giant bridge and she looked up at the towering structure, her gut clenched. Her phobia would have made more sense if she'd experienced some sort of terrible trauma involving a bridge. But there was nothing she could recall. She'd tried using a therapist who specialized in hypnotism to dig into her buried memories. Again, *nada*.

Beside her, Tucker exhaled a sigh. "She's a beaut, ain't she?"

"The bridge?"

"A marvel of engineering, you betcha. She takes my breath away." His gaze turned misty as he stared upward. "A couple of weeks ago, we had the annual Great Columbia Crossing, which is the only day in the year when the bridge is closed to vehicles and opened to pedestrians. My wife and I used to cross every year, holding hands and grinning like a couple of tourists."

She looked toward the short, round man who leaned heavily on his cane. He was adorable. A charmer. As cute as his tugboat. "You're an expert on the history of this area."

"You betcha."

"What do you remember about the Lightkeeper?"

"When those murders were happening, that was all anybody could talk about. Some people blamed it on the supernatural, like sea monsters coming ashore or the ghosts of drowned sailors. Others claimed to have seen aliens. Since I'm into landmarks, I tried to figure out why he went to lighthouses."

"And why do you think he did?"

"A symbolic thing. A lighthouse is a good place to hide. Or a fortress to give tactical advantage over an enemy attack. Maybe the Lightkeeper wanted to keep a flame burning to commemorate his evil deeds." Tucker shrugged. "I can't explain how Dagmar's mama found the right curse to make him stop. I don't want to think she was a witch."

"There are good witches."

"I suppose."

She remembered Jake's hostile reaction to the idea that his aunt had been a witch. "Did Jake ever talk about it?"

"He sure did. Got all tangled up in the mystery when he was a kid. We used to call him Boy Detective." Tucker barked a laugh. "None of us—not even his dad—thought he'd join the police when he grew up."

As they drew closer to the Astoria shoreline, Tucker the tour guide automatically pointed out various sights, ranging from the coast guard station to the waterfront trolley. When his redheaded niece carefully guided the tug into the marina, Skylar saw Jake waiting for her on the pier, and her heart took a little jump. Bringing herself under control, she did some deep breathing and employed the compartmentalizing techniques she learned at Quantico when practicing with firearms or attending an autopsy. *Concentrate.* She knew how to turn her attention away from one problem and focus on another.

It worked on everything except her phobia.

And Jake.

"Are you okay?" Tucker asked.

She realized that her nostrils had flared. And she was probably blushing. *This won't do.* She smiled at the old sailor. "Thanks for the ride."

"Anytime. I don't have a regular schedule this time of year, so my tug can always respond." He tilted his head to the side. "I think you're going to be good for Jake. He needs someone special."

And so do I.

"I'M NOT GOING in there by myself." Jake looked beyond Skylar in the passenger seat to see the front window of Delilah's Beauty Salon, decorated with hanging baskets of fake foliage—vines and pink azaleas. "We should start at the Sand Bar, questioning witnesses about Lucille Dixon."

"We're already here, and it's not even eleven o'clock. The bar might not be open." Her mouth twitched as though holding back laughter. "Don't worry, Samson. She won't cut your hair and zap your strength."

"Why me and not you?"

"Because you know everybody in town, and the ladies will talk to you."

If Skylar hadn't been so cute, he would have flat-out refused. But she seemed like a different woman after their kiss and her ride on the tug. Gone was the kickass special agent. This version of Skylar wore a smile. For the first time since they met, she actually seemed happy.

"Okay, I'll go in there," he said. "But you owe me."

"Fine with me. How should I pay you back?"

The unwanted but very much appreciated image of Skylar lying naked in his bed with her glossy auburn hair spread across the pillow popped up in his mind. "I'll think of something."

He shut down his imagination before entering the salon, not wanting to project his lust for Skylar at the five women who fluttered around the adjustable-height barber chairs and studied themselves in the wall-to-wall mirrors. The scent of perfumed shampoo and fancy products mingled with the chemical smell of the disinfectant used to sanitize combs and such. The colors on the walls and countertops were pink, black, white and pinker.

He approached the bleached blonde at the front counter who presided over a glass case filled with lotions and potions and fancy barrettes.

"I'm looking for Delilah," he said. Dagmar had mentioned the salon owner's magenta hair, and he didn't see anyone matching that description. "Is she in today?"

His deep baritone echoed through the salon and silenced the *snip-snip* and the background music of Taylor Swift on the radio. All the women stopped what they were doing and stared. He was a dab of testosterone in a sea of estrogen. A fish out of water. A bull in a—

"Jake Armstrong!" A blonde stylist with a Mohawk whirled away from the head of hair she'd been clipping and stalked toward him. "You remember me, don't you?"

Not really. He took a stab in the dark. "From high school?"

"We were in the same chem class with Pyro Pierce. I'm Chloe."

He couldn't avoid her snuggle without being rude. And the hug wasn't all bad. She had standout breasts. "Chloe O'Connor. Coco." He stepped away from her. "I'd like to chat, but I'm here on police business."

"I know," she gushed. "The Shadowkeeper. Gawd, so awful."

"I need to talk to Delilah."

"She's out for the rest of the morning," Coco said. "Over at her boyfriend's house."

"Joe Rogers?"

"Yep." Coco bobbed her head, which somehow caused her cleavage to bounce. "They've been going out for a couple of years, and I don't know why she doesn't marry the guy."

A stylist with short, spiky turquoise hair piped up. "Could be because she's already married."

"Separated," Coco corrected. "Her almost ex-husband is also dating."

"Whatever. I heard that Delilah's son hates Rogers."

Much as Jake disliked gossip, it was a good way to pick up info. "What's her son's name? How old is he?"

"Trevor Miller," said Coco. "Kind of a hottie, but too young for me. Just eighteen."

Not too young to be the Shadowkeeper. Jake didn't know how this detail fit into the investigation, but he'd keep young Trevor in mind.

"If you ask me," said the woman at the receptionist's desk, "it's not Delilah who's avoiding marriage. Did you ever see photos of Rogers's first wife? She was a fashion model from Houston. Tall and gorgeous and totally out of Delilah's league."

"I heard she married some millionaire rancher after she dumped Rogers," Coco said. "A real cowboy who rides horses and shoots six-guns. Do you know how to ride, Jake?"

He steered back to the main topic, recalling something Rogers had told them. "She divorced the rancher and married again. Moved to Paris, France."

Coco rolled her eyes. "Some women have all the luck."

"She's supposed to be a designer," said a gray-haired woman who sat in one of the barber chairs. "I remember her swooping around town in leopard prints and blouses cut down to her belly button."

"Did her son go with her to Paris?" he asked.

"Don't think so," Coco said.

Turquoise Hair spoke up. "Joe Rogers's son, Bradley, split his time between here and Texas when he was in school. I went out with him in high school. Only once, but that still counts."

"Tell me about him," he said.

"Nerdy but kind of macho at the same time, always talking about how women need to be treated like princesses. Hah!"

Jake's ears pricked up. "Did he use that word? Princess?"

She wiggled her fingers in front of his face, showing off her lavender manicure. "Called me his Purple Princess. Because it's one of my fave colors."

"Have you heard from Bradley recently? Is he in town?"

"We lost touch."

Jake would make finding Bradley Rogers's current address and phone number a priority. After a few more moments, he extricated himself from the salon, rushed across the sidewalk and dove into the driver's seat of the Explorer. He pulled away from the curb before the ladies in Delilah's could peek out the window and wonder about Skylar in the passenger seat.

She ended her phone call and turned to him. "How did it go?"

"I hate rumors."

"Me, too."

"Everybody has a story. Most aren't verifiable."

"Much like questioning witnesses," she said. "We hear biased opinions more than facts."

"I never saw Delilah," he said. "She's supposed to be at Rogers's place, which is where we're going right now. But I did get a couple of ideas. Delilah has a son—a hottie according to Coco, a woman I knew in high school—and he doesn't like Rogers."

"I'm not following," she said. "How does that apply to the Shadowkeeper?"

"Her son—his name is Trevor—might be trying to frame Rogers by taking his car and leaving it outside Phoebe's apartment. Making it look like Rogers was the stalker."

"Flimsy," she decreed. "What else did you find out?"

"Bradley, Rogers's son, divided his time between his parents. His mom had custody, and he mostly lived with her in Houston. But he came for long visits, enough that he was enrolled in the Astoria high school. One of the women in the salon dated him and said he called women princesses."

Her green eyes widened like a snowy owl, and she leaned across the console to give his arm a tap. "Good job, Gossip Girl."

"The way I figure, Bradley is twenty-seven or twenty-eight. His childhood was disrupted by the Lightkeeper who threatened him and his mom, causing his mother to move him away from Astoria. Plus, he could have known both victims in Texas."

"And he thinks of women as princesses. A significant clue. Our best chance at solving this thing is breaking down the Shadowkeeper's messages. He's telling more than he realizes."

His downfall. "He needs to be stopped before tonight."

She waggled her phone at him. "I heard from Crawford about the traffic cams on either end of the bridge. They show license plates and a glimpse of the driver, but last night was too foggy to make an identification."

"Did Lucille's car cross last night?"

"A red Kia. At 1:17 in the morning, which was probably after she left the Sand Bar, her Kia entered the Astoria side of the bridge. The camera never showed her car returning."

He drew a logical conclusion. "Which means the Kia is still on the Washington side."

"Crawford already put out a BOLO and sent a team to look for it."

Considering the camera footage, he tried to picture the

sequence of events. Either Lucille drove herself across the bridge and met her killer, or he rode with her in the Kia. Or he waited for her at the lighthouse in his own vehicle, killed her and then moved both cars. "Something doesn't add up."

"It gets worse. I'm sorry, Jake."

"Were any of our other suspects on the bridge last night?"

"Actually, yes." She turned her head, avoiding his gaze. "There's not much traffic late at night, and the camera guys analyzed speeds, patterns and timing from the footage. A fifteen-year-old Toyota crossed from Astoria at 12:22 and returned at 3:45, which would place the driver at the light-house at the right time."

"Who was it?"

"Alan Quilling."

Jake had almost forgotten about his forensic tech as a suspect. Not a smart investigative tactic. They were *all* under suspicion, and Quilling had just moved to the front of the line.

Chapter Seventeen

On the street where Rogers lived, the Explorer parked in front of an unmarked car with a person in the driver's seat. While Jake checked in with the officer on stakeout, Skylar got out of the car and looked toward the newspaper editor's house.

The unusually sunny day showed a well-maintained Craftsman home in pale yellow with white trim and a porch across the front. In the side yard, a neglected wooden swing set with a plastic slide hadn't fared so well. The weathered crossbars showed damage from years of exposure in the damp climate. The slide tilted at an awkward angle. And the chains on the swing were rusted. An eyesore. A painful reminder that children no longer played here. Rogers's son hadn't lived with his dad for a very long time.

Jake returned to her side. "The officer on stakeout says Rogers's purple-haired girlfriend came over a couple of hours ago for breakfast."

"Magenta, not purple. Is he certain Rogers didn't leave the house?"

"Not on his watch. He's been here since 3:15 a.m., and the guy before him swears nobody left or entered. They're inexperienced and could be mistaken, but…" The police stakeout gave Rogers a decent alibi for last night. "Do we really need to talk to him again?"

Even if he wasn't the Shadowkeeper, she wasn't about to

let Rogers off the hook. Not when she sensed that he was up to something. He'd initially lied about his alibi and gave flimsy excuses for why his car was parked outside Phoebe's house. "I want to get his son's contact information."

"Okay." He shuffled from foot to foot. "Let's not stay long. I'm anxious to talk to Quilling and find out why he drove across the bridge last night."

She and Jake approached the front porch as Rogers and an attractive, middle-aged woman with bobbed magenta hair exited. Her frank grin and straightforward attitude made a positive first impression on Skylar who stuck out her hand. "You must be Delilah Miller."

"And you must be that female fed everybody is yakking about." Graciously, Delilah accepted the handshake. "Come by my salon, honey, and I'll touch up those highlights."

"We've already been to your shop," she said. "And my hair color is natural."

"Well, aren't you the lucky one."

"Can we come in?" Jake asked.

"Buzz off," Rogers said rudely. "I'm leaving."

Jake centered his considerable bulk in the middle of the sidewalk, blocking access to the driveway where Rogers's black sedan was parked. "We're getting a search warrant."

The newsman's heavy eyebrows lowered into a scowl. His outthrust jaw locked, and his complexion flushed red in a burst of anger. "When are you going to catch on, Armstrong? We're on the same damn side. I need to get to the *Sun* and make sure everything is running smoothly. The Shadowkeeper sent another email."

"We're aware," Jake said.

"We don't have time for another damn interrogation. As for the search warrant, I'd advise against it and so would my lawyer. I'm not letting you in my house when I'm not here."

"I'll stay." Delilah volunteered.

"Thank you for your cooperation," Skylar said.

Delilah gave a pleasant smile. "The important thing is finding this horrible Shadow person who is killing young women. We'll do anything we can to help."

Rogers's hostility faded as he gazed at her. "You're a good woman, Delilah, but you don't understand. These two idiots suspect me."

"And a search will prove you did nothing wrong. That way they can get back to the real business of solving these crimes." She kissed him on the cheek. "Go to work, Joe. I'll lock up when I leave."

Their casual interaction seemed average and innocent to Skylar. They came across as a normal couple in their prime. Likewise, the interior of his home was neatly decorated with pottery, wood carvings and house plants. Nothing spectacular. Nothing suspicious. The scent of coffee and bacon hung in the air.

"Might as well get this over with," Jake said to Delilah. "Where were you the night before last?"

Delilah pointed down the hall. "In the bedroom. Joe and I watched the late news to check the weather forecast, which was—no surprise—cloudy and wet. Then we rolled over and went to sleep."

"That gives Rogers an alibi," he said.

"If you're serious about searching, I expect you'll want to take a gander at Joe's files and paperwork," she said. "His office is the first door on the left."

"Thank you, ma'am."

"It's Delilah," she said. "I'm not sure we've met, but I know you, Jake Armstrong."

"How's that… Delilah?"

"Astoria is a small town, and you're hard to miss."

Jake disappeared into the office, but Skylar stayed put.

Still curious about the alibi, she asked, "Why didn't Rogers want to tell us that you spent the night?"

"He's old-fashioned." Her laughter sounded like something between a giggle and a snort. "That old goofball worries about my reputation, even though I've been separated for five years and live in my own house with my son. He's the real reason I haven't married Joe."

"Your son," Skylar said, watching for a reaction. "Trevor."

Delilah showed the first signs of real alarm. "Why does the FBI know his name? He's not in trouble, is he?"

Purposefully, Skylar didn't directly answer the question, allowing the other woman's worries to fester. "You said Trevor was the real reason you haven't married Joe. Why?"

"He's a teenage boy." Delilah's lower lip trembled. Her fear hadn't receded. "I guess I should start calling him a man. Has he done something wrong, broken the law?"

"We heard his name from the stylists in the shop." Skylar cocked her head to one side. "Does he often get into trouble?"

"Not a bit." Delilah fluttered her hand, showing off a gorgeous manicure that matched her hair. "Anyway, he disliked Joe from the minute we started dating. Not because of anything Joe did, mind you. It's about me. Trevor is jealous of my attention. Know what I mean?"

Though she had no children of her own, Skylar recognized the pattern. Young men often became overly attached to their mothers. "Must be difficult for you."

"If I married Joe, my son would be super upset. Right now, he's being a good kid, taking classes at the local college and working before he decides what he wants to do with his life. After that, he'll probably move out." She blinked away a tear. "I'll miss him."

"Is he friendly with Bradley Rogers?"

"Joe's son?" Delilah shook her head. "I've only seen him a handful of times. A good-looking kid, real tall. Not as big as Jake, but much taller than his daddy. Probably gets it from his mom who used to be a model. She's almost six feet."

"What does Trevor think of him?"

"First time they met, a couple of years ago, he looked Bradley up online. Found out that his mom upgraded with her second husband. A Texas rancher with gobs of money. Trevor was impressed, but not me. That cowboy isn't cool. In every photo, he's packing a gun."

Skylar would have been more concerned if their victims had been shot. "The second husband was different from Joe Rogers."

"I'll say. My Joe is grumpy but has a heart of gold. He's thoughtful and funny. He'd never hurt a flea. The cowboy looks like a badass." Delilah fluffed her hair. "Trevor mentioned Bradley's scars from supposed 'accidents.' I think he was abused."

Skylar made a mental note to follow up on this accusation. Many a serial killer had a background of childhood abuse. "Is Bradley living here in Astoria?"

"Wish I could tell you, honey, but I don't know. Joe hasn't mentioned it."

"He went to high school here," Skylar said, recalling what Jake had told her. "At least part of the time when his parents were sharing custody."

"That must have been eight or nine years ago. Well before Joe and I were a thing."

"Do you have a phone number and address for Bradley?"

Delilah took her phone from her purse and scrolled. "This is the most recent. Used it to send him an online gift card for his birthday a couple of weeks ago, so it's probably current."

After Skylar downloaded the information—which included a Houston, Texas, address—she looked up and saw Jake coming down the hall. His timing couldn't have been more perfect if he'd been listening through the open door for the moment when she had the addy and phone. Probably, he had been eavesdropping. He was itching to talk with Quilling.

"I'm done," he announced. "You've been real helpful, Delilah."

"Anytime, cutie pie."

She ushered them to the door. While Delilah locked up, Jake bounded down the two steps from the porch and hurried toward the Explorer. Skylar understood his eagerness to deal with Quilling. The tall, skinny head of APD's forensic department was part of the team, and—as a marine—Jake would follow the code of loyalty: never leave one of your soldiers behind.

As soon as she fastened her seat belt, he said, "We need a forensic person to process Quilling's Toyota for trace evidence, and I can't use someone who works with him. Will you arrange for an FBI tech who is in town putting up cameras to meet us at Quilling's apartment?"

She bobbed her head. "I can do that."

"Forensics can tell us if Lucille was in the car with him." He winced. "Or in the trunk."

She wished she could reassure him, but Quilling had twice popped up in compromising circumstances. He had to be considered a suspect. She pulled out her phone and started making calls to find a tech.

By the time she made plans with a team of FBI forensic experts who had just installed closed-circuit cameras outside a restaurant with a twelve-foot-tall lighthouse replica, the Explorer arrived at a rectangular, three-story apartment building with all the charm of a shoebox. In the parking lot, she saw a beat-up, gray, late model Toyota sedan. "Is that Quilling's car?"

"He's not into vehicles."

She figured as much. Though trying not to stereotype, she suspected the nerdy guy in round eyeglasses spent all his extra cash on computers and electronic equipment. Before getting out of the car, she said, "I'll stay here and wait for the FBI tech. If you bring me Quilling's car keys, we can get started with the processing right away."

"I appreciate the chance to talk to him alone," Jake said. "I want you to know that I agreed with your reprimand about the sloppy way he handled evidence. If you hadn't sent him home, I would have."

She believed him. Still, she recognized his concern for a guy he had trusted and worked with. "What would you have done if I hadn't found that photo of him with Phoebe?"

He exhaled in a whoosh. "I probably would have put him back to work. This investigation is testing the limits of the APD. We just don't have all that many officers."

She reached across the console and rested her hand on his arm. "I hope Quilling has a good explanation for why he went to Cape Disappointment last night."

He caught her hand and brought it to his lips for a quick kiss. "I'm hoping the same thing."

AT THE FRONT ENTRANCE, Jake followed another resident into the building, so he didn't need to use the buzzer before he hiked up to apartment 306 at the rear.

Though he and Quilling were friendly, he'd never been here. When people got together after work, they usually came to Jake's bungalow at the edge of the forest—a fixer-upper he bought when he left the marines. His first project was to add a huge cedar deck with a grill for cooking meat outside.

He tapped his knuckles against the door. "It's Jake Armstrong. Open up."

In seconds, the door swung wide. Dressed in grungy, baggy, mismatched sweats from head to toe with his hair uncombed and splotches of stubble on his pointed chin, Quilling looked like he'd just crawled out of bed. "Good morning, Armstrong."

"It's almost noon."

Jake pushed the door aside and entered the typical bachelor pad furnished with a worn sofa and two matching chairs, probably from his parents' house, unopened mail on the desk, lots of clutter, a fifty-five-inch flat-screen TV and an impressive computer setup for gaming. A pile of empty pizza boxes and beer bottles attested to Quilling's less-than-healthy diet. On the computer screen was a video game with flying dragons blowing fire down upon a medieval village.

Quilling darkened the screen and muted the sound. "Would you like a beer?"

Jake squinted at the label. "Is that a lighthouse?"

"What? No, it's brewed here in Astoria, and that's supposed to be the historic column at the top of Coxcomb Hill— our famous landmark."

Jake cut to the chase. "What the hell were you doing on the bridge last night?"

"I wasn't on the bridge."

"Don't lie to me. We have footage from the traffic cams that show your car crossing to Cape Disappointment at 12:22 and returning at 3:45."

"I swear, I was here. Had a few beers. Played my video game and went to bed."

"What time?"

"I don't remember. After one or one-thirty, for sure."

"Did anyone see you? Maybe a clerk at the store where you bought your beer. Does your computer have a system to show what time you're playing?"

Quilling took a long chug from the beer. "You're asking me for an alibi."

Damn right. "Give me your car keys so I can give them

to Agent Gambel. We need to process your vehicle for trace evidence."

"Evidence of what?"

"There was a second victim last night." Quilling was probably the only person in town who didn't know. "Killed at the North Head Lighthouse."

The blood drained from his face. He swallowed hard, pushed his glasses up on his nose and staggered toward a shelf by the door. Not saying a word, he held out his key ring.

Jake grabbed it and went to the window overlooking the parking lot. He spotted Skylar in her official-looking suit. She'd been joined by the two musclebound techs who lowered the body at the North Head Lighthouse. He unlocked the apartment window, then shoved the glass and the screen open. Waving to Skylar, he dangled the car keys. Before she could refuse, he tossed the key chain down to her.

She easily made the catch, which somehow satisfied him. Then she gave a thumbs-up.

He swung around and focused on Quilling who had collapsed into an indented place on the sofa which had to be where he usually sat. The guy was pathetic. Hard to picture him as the brazen Shadowkeeper—a narcissist who posed his victims and sent taunting notes to the police.

Jake stalked into the adjoining kitchen. "I'm making coffee."

"You don't have to do that."

"It's for you, Quilling. You need to get sober fast because I want you to use your brain." Taking him into custody would be embarrassing. "I don't want to arrest you."

Quilling bolted to his feet. Apparently, the thought of being on the wrong side of the jail bars galvanized him into action. He picked his way through the clutter into the kitchen and took over the process of making coffee in one of those machines with the pods. Clearing his throat, he spun around to face Jake. "Go ahead, Detective. Ask me anything."

"Let's start with Phoebe Conway. Tell me about your relationship with her."

"One-sided." Quilling pushed his floppy brown hair off his forehead. "She asked me to take some publicity photos of her. Even though it was an obvious ruse to get inside information from me for an article about the burglar who hit seven houses in a week, I agreed. She was friendly and so pretty. Way out of my league."

"You must have been tempted to tell her about the leads we had on the robberies."

"Tempted, yes." Quilling took his full coffee cup, carried it to a kitchen table piled high with clutter and sat in a straight-backed chair. "But I didn't say a word. I know better than to talk to a reporter. Coffee for you?"

"I'm fine."

"Why are you asking me about Phoebe? It was only a couple of hours."

"When Special Agent Gambel searched Phoebe's apartment, she found a photo of you in an embrace with her. Explain."

He slurped his coffee as though it was the magic elixir he needed to win his imaginary battle with the dragons. "She wanted me to show her how to set the camera to take a photo five seconds after she posed for it. Her equipment didn't have that feature, but mine did. So, I illustrated. When I got into position, I didn't expect for her to hug me like that."

"But you didn't mind," Jake said.

"I won't lie. It was nice."

"Do you have an alibi for the night she was killed?"

"Wasting time with Phoebe put me behind in my regular duties. I had to work late at the forensic lab. Didn't leave until after midnight." Behind his glasses, his eyes teared up. "Who was killed last night?"

"Lucille Dixon."

"The cowgirl who sang at the Sand Bar? The 'Your Cheatin' Heart' girl? Damn." Quilling seemed genuinely upset.

For a few minutes, they talked about their memories of Lucille. When Quilling mentioned the note he'd found on Phoebe's phone, Jake refused to discuss the case with him. His phone buzzed in his pocket. It was Skylar.

"You can stop interrogating Quilling," she said.

Relief spread through him. "That's good news."

"The techs found evidence. A hair."

Jake didn't understand. Typically, a hair would be run through all kinds of tests to determine DNA and all the rest of the forensic stuff. "How do you know who it belongs to?"

"It's magenta. Not purple, magenta. And it was in the passenger seat."

Jake drew the logical conclusion. Delilah had been riding in Quilling's car, and her fiancé was the driver.

Quilling was off the hook.

Chapter Eighteen

After reassuring Quilling and ordering him not to leave his apartment, Jake joined Skylar and the forensic techs in the parking lot. Given Quilling's position in the APD, the techs agreed to transport the aged Toyota to Portland for further tests. Though the dashboard and steering wheel had been wiped down, four different sets of fingerprints, including Quilling's, had been collected. Three magenta hairs had been found.

Leaving them to do their jobs, Jake got back into the Explorer with Skylar. She tapped the face of the black titanium field watch she always wore. "It's almost two o'clock. If we hope to make it to the autopsy in Warrenton by three, we should leave now."

"Our time is better spent here," he said. "We need to talk to people at the Sand Bar. To come up with a timeline for last night and find out who Lucille was talking to. Not to mention, who she'd been dating."

"When we get a list of suspects," she said, "we'll compare Lucille's boyfriends with Tabitha's list for Phoebe."

He started the car and pulled out of the parking area. Unanswered questions rattled around in his brain. He started with the most perplexing. "What the hell was Delilah doing in Quilling's car?"

"In the passenger seat," she reminded him.

"Which probably means Rogers was driving." The newspaper editor might have needed a different car to cross the bridge last night because his little black sedan was already compromised. But why Quilling? They didn't live in the same neighborhood. "There's got to be a connection."

"And we'd better find it," she said. "We'll skip the autopsy. I spoke to Crawford a few minutes ago. He and Jimi Kim will be with the medical examiner, and they'll give us the conclusions. He said it wasn't necessary for us to attend in person."

"We can start at the Sand Bar. Get lunch."

"Yes," said the woman who loved to eat.

He did a celebratory fist pump. "Food *and* interviewing witnesses. Two birds, one stone. Sand Bar makes a decent clam chowder."

"Back to the main topic. Delilah in Quilling's car. She might have been riding with Quilling. But I can't imagine they're friends. I doubt he goes to her salon. His hair doesn't look like it gets special attention from a stylist."

Jake raked his fingers through his own short hair. Most of the APD officers, including Dot, used a barber shop around the corner from headquarters. "Quilling is too old to have gone to high school with Delilah's son. He's more like Bradley Rogers's age."

"And we don't even know if Bradley is in town." She looked down at her phone screen. "I could call the phone number Delilah gave me. But I'd rather figure out where he lives and visit him unannounced."

"An ambush."

"Exactly."

"Finding out if he's in Astoria and where he's staying sounds like a job for Chief Kim. Give her a call."

While she contacted the APD command central, he considered questions that should be asked at the Sand Bar. The bartenders tended to keep watch over the inebriated patrons to prevent fights from breaking out. Had they noticed any-one suspicious? Anyone approaching Lucille? Yesterday, he'd spoken to a couple of the regular employees about Ty McKenna's alibi, and they'd been cooperative.

Skylar finished up her phone call at about the same time as he made a right turn into the parking lot for the waterfront tavern and restaurant. Not a place he'd ordinarily go to get a meal. Apart from the chowder, their menu was burgers and anything deep fried. The Sand Bar was—as it said in the name—a bar. With an impressive selection of craft beers.

Before they left the Explorer, she briefed him. "Chief Kim is doing a search for Bradley Rogers's local address. Most of the surveillance cameras have been placed near lighthouses and are sending their simultaneous broadcasts to a big-screen computer at APD. The chief compared it to one of those on-line meeting places with locations instead of faces. The sites are also available on many phone screens—including yours and mine—through a special app." She shook her head. "I'm always amazed at what the electronics guys can do."

"Which lighthouses aren't covered?"

"Terrible Tilly on the offshore island isn't, because get-ting there is too complicated. And not Cape Meares, which is farthest away in the opposite direction from Cape Disap-pointment."

"And has already been used." He leaned across the console toward her and inhaled the vanilla and citrus fragrance he'd come to associate with Skylar. She smelled like the Dream-sicle ice cream bars he'd loved as a kid. "Show me the app."

On her phone, she tapped an icon and brought up a pic-ture of the lighthouse replica at the miniature golf course where a worker in a dark green polo shirt was hosing down sidewalks. "When we leave the bar, we should go there. The Shadowkeeper pointed us in that direction with his clues."

He didn't like the idea of taking directions from a serial

killer, but the communication from the Shadowkeeper couldn't be ignored. He had clearly indicated the North Head Lighthouse in his text to Skylar. "From his messages, it seems like he knows something about the women he kills. He stalks them. What's his trigger? Why did he select Phoebe and Lucille?"

When he left the Explorer, she walked beside him through the pleasantly sunlit day. "Victimology," she said. "One of my fave topics."

"But you're not one of those people who tries to get inside the killer's head, are you?"

She shuddered. "Can't think of a more repulsive place to be. But I like to speculate about what comes next. Both Phoebe and Lucille are attractive women in highly visible professions. Local celebrities."

A simple but accurate description. "He keeps mentioning Phoebe and her column. And I expect we'll see more comments about the songbird, which has to be Lucille. And maybe about you, Skylar. You're pretty. And everybody in town knows who you are now."

"I certainly don't think of myself as a celebrity, but the Shadowkeeper has targeted me. He's sent a text directly to my phone. Makes me wonder if I could be used as bait to draw him out."

"Not exactly regulation FBI protocol."

"Protocol," she said, "is whatever works."

THE ENTRANCE TO the Sand Bar featured rough, unvarnished wood siding and two porthole-shaped windows with brass fittings. The theme, Skylar guessed, was a shipwreck in the bay.

Only a handful of patrons were scattered at the dark wood tables. Later in the evening, she supposed, a full band would take the stage, and the dance floor would be hopping. The interior lighting came from dim, flickering lantern fixtures, but several large windows lined the wall overlooking the harbor. The atmosphere tried for a cool vibe, but the mood today was decidedly somber.

A blond waitress with red-rimmed eyes gestured to the tables. "Sit wherever you want."

As soon as they settled at a window, a dark, bearded guy built like a fireplug pulled up a chair and made it a threesome. "We got to catch this bastard, Jake. For Lucille."

"Sam Henderson is the owner. Sam, this is Special Agent Skylar Gambel. We're investigating."

He gave her a nod. "Order anything you want. Both of you. It's on the house."

After deciding on chowder and a cheeseburger, she mentioned Ty McKenna. "He was here on Tuesday night until closing time."

"Ty's sober, but I appreciate him being designated driver for his hard-drinking friends. Tuesday is usually quiet. Not a big night for us." His face crumpled, and he looked down at his stubby fingers as they twisted in his lap. "Lucille was singing. Early in the evening, McKenna did his best to pick her up, but she wasn't interested."

"Had he dated her before?" Skylar asked.

Henderson frowned and stroked his beard, trying to remember. "I don't think so. Lucille might have been a world-class flirt and would let anybody buy her a beer, but she didn't actually date many guys."

The shorter the list, the fewer suspects they had to check out. "Tell me about her current boyfriend. Or boyfriends. Has she recently broken up with anybody?"

"To hear her tell it, Lucille never ended a relationship until she had a good reason. You know, it was always 'Your Cheatin' Heart' with her boyfriends." He tapped the tabletop to emphasize his point. "She's been dating the guitar player who works here on Thursday and the weekend. He'll be in at four and plays until eight. He and Lucille were making a demo tape."

Skylar jotted down his name and phone number, just in case the guitarist didn't show. While she'd been talking to Henderson, Jake was fielding questions from others on the staff and the sad-eyed waitress. Though they might be more inclined to talk in a group setting, Skylar didn't like to conduct interviews with more than one person at a time. She separated the waitress, Jillian, from the herd and went outside with her.

Jillian, dressed in snug jeans, a tiny apron and a Sand Bar T-shirt, lit up a cigarette and strolled to the edge of the walkway above the Columbia. The smell of freshly caught fish from the docks mixed with the oily, mechanical stink from motorized vessels. Casual waves splashed against the pier while terns and gulls made their own racket. Low, drifting clouds hadn't yet masked the glare from the sun.

In the daylight, the wrinkles around Jillian's big, blue eyes were more visible. At one time, Skylar guessed, the waitress had been as cute as a Kewpie doll, and she was still an attractive woman.

Jillian exhaled a cloud of smoke and said, "Lucille and I used to come out here a couple of times every night. To get away from the loud, handsy jerks in the bar. She was a sweet kid. I'll miss her."

"Henderson mentioned a boyfriend," Skylar prompted.

"Xander the guitar player." She combed her fingers through her shoulder-length blond hair. "A nice-looking dude, if you like them tall and skinny."

"Was that her type?"

"You bet. Soulful eyes and messy hair."

Skylar knew who fit that description. "Did she date Alan Quilling?"

"The nerd who works for the APD in forensics? Lucille didn't date him, but he's somebody she might find interesting."

On a hunch, Skylar asked, "What about Bradley Rogers?"

"In his dreams." Jillian inhaled and exhaled quickly. "He's

been in here a couple of times recently, shooting off his mouth about how everything's bigger and better in Texas. And comparing the size of his cowboy boots with Lucille's. He'd dance the two-step with her, and accidentally-on-purpose grab her bottom. She slapped him."

Though Skylar hadn't come face-to-face with Bradley, he was beginning to look better and better as a suspect. "Did Henderson throw him out?"

"He said he was sorry, and we cut him some slack because his dad is the guy who runs the *Sun*. Joe Rogers has always been good to the Sand Bar. We advertise with him." Her gasp sounded like the beginning of a sob. "A shame about that reporter who worked for him. Phoebe."

"Did she know Lucille?"

"Know her? She wrote a whole article with photographs about how talented she was. Called her a songbird."

That must have been where the *songbird* label got started. Figuring she was on a roll, Skylar asked, "Did Lucille ever date Trevor Miller?"

"Delilah's son. Gawd, no. He's not even old enough to drink. Dyed his buzz cut hair in a red-and-blue checkerboard pattern. He's cute but not for dating." She put out her cigarette and tucked it into a little pouch to dispose of later. "I adore his mom. She's the genius behind my highlights that totally cover the gray."

"Anything else you can tell me about Bradley Rogers? Do you know where he lives? I want to get ahold of him."

"After he tried making the moves on Lucille, he started in on me. He's a major, major jerkwad. Of course, I shut him down. But before I did, he told me we could spend the night in the best hotel in Astoria, soak in a hot tub and have a spa treatment."

"I'm new in town. Which hotel is that?"

"The Pierpoint—a crazy expensive, gorgeous place.

Every room has a balcony and a view. I'd love to stay there and wallow in luxury." Jillian pivoted to face the Sand Bar, which would never be defined as luxurious. "But not if it means spending time with that creep."

"You've been a help," Skylar said. "Thanks for talking to me."

"I'll do anything to help catch the monster who killed Lucille." Jillian cringed. "You don't think it was Bradley, do you?"

"He's a person of interest."

Back inside the Sand Bar, Skylar stood at the horseshoe bar and took out her phone to call Crawford. He had given her a great deal of leeway during this investigation, but she still wanted her mentor's expert judgment.

Her wristwatch showed 3:07. Too early for the autopsy to be over. She left Crawford a message to call her. The time was 3:11. Minutes dragged like hours, but time passed too quickly. They needed results. She feared the Shadowkeeper would strike again in spite of the surveillance cameras. Her ride on the tugboat—though a wonderful relief—had been a time waste. And here she and Jake were at the Sand Bar eating dinner.

A burst of laughter from the table where Jake and three other guys sat caught her attention. Two of them held pool cues. An adjoining room had three tables. A glance told Skylar that none of these men would have appealed to Lucille. Not her type at all.

Do I have a type? She returned Jake's wave but didn't rush across the restaurant to join him. Most of the guys she dated were athletic. All of them were smart. Twice, she'd lived with men. Both were dark-haired, professional and fit well into any setting or situation. They blended. Not like Jake.

He stood out. Clearly, she would notice this tall, muscular Viking with the slow, sexy smile and blazing blue eyes.

A near-perfect physical specimen. Of course, she was drawn to him. Evolutionary theory indicated that women sought males who would produce strong, healthy babies. But the ripple of excitement flowing through her veins felt like more than natural selection or hormones, more than pure animal attraction…or maybe not. Maybe lust was enough.

She didn't really have time to consider her romantic prospects. First order of business: find Bradley Rogers. She called Chief Kim to see if she'd discovered where he lived. His permanent address was in Houston, but he was having mail forwarded to a box at a postal service center in town. That was where her trail ended. No trace of Bradley in Astoria or any of the other nearby towns.

Skylar said, "I heard that he might be staying at the Pierpoint Hotel."

"How very bougie," the chief said. "I didn't know he had that kind of money. I'll check with the front desk and get back to you."

When she turned away from the bar, Skylar came face-to-face with Dagmar and a man with a long ponytail who had to be Pyro Pierce, the science teacher. With all of Dagmar's flowing scarves and Pierce's Sasquatch T-shirt and denim jacket, they reminded her of pictures of hippies from the 1960s. Their height difference—with Dagmar in platform heels that gave her a good six inches on him—was endearing.

"We've come to help," Dagmar said.

Their offer was wrong on so many different levels. They were citizens. Untrained and untested. If they were hurt— God forbid—Skylar and the FBI would be liable. Jake wanted his cousin kept apart from the investigation. Crawford certainly wouldn't approve. Still…

"Cool," Skylar said.

Chapter Nineteen

Dagmar introduced her beau in a fond drawl that sounded like slow motion, which was probably because Skylar was so driven. Everything needed to sped up. She recalled what Jake had said about Pierce. "You're a science teacher."

"Guilty." He had a nice smile and a healthy glow. A bicycle rider, Pierce had given them their first clue when he noticed Rogers's black sedan parked outside the apartment house where Phoebe lived.

"You might be able to help me. Did you ever have Joe Rogers's son, Bradley, in class?"

"I did." His eyebrows pulled together over his glasses. "Bradley wasn't a pleasant kid. Not an atypical personality for an adolescent with raging hormones, but Bradley was worse than most. I think the technical term is…creepy."

Jillian had called him a jerkwad. Apparently, he hadn't mellowed since high school. "How so?"

"In chemistry class, he showed intense interest in how to rig a bomb for maximum casualties. In biology, he loved dissecting the frogs and earthworms. Kept asking if we could get a human cadaver and promised his rich stepfather would pay for it."

"Dark," Dagmar said. "I'd probably like him."

"No, luv. You have nothing in common with him." When he looked at her, his face lit up. "You study the macabre as a learning experience. Bradley wanted to hurt other people."

An interesting perspective. Before she could say more, Skylar's phone buzzed, and she excused herself to answer.

The usually even-tempered Chief Kim sounded irritated. "Sorry, Skylar, I couldn't get much info from that snobby woman at the Pierpoint front desk. Leah Fairchild, not so fair in my opinion. All she'd tell me was that no person named Bradley Rogers was currently registered. And then she refused to answer any other questions."

"What did you ask?" Skylar asked.

"If she knew Bradley from when he was growing up. Or if he'd used a different name." She huffed a sigh of pure exasperation. "If you go over there and flash your FBI badge, that snooty woman might cooperate. She likes authority figures."

"But that applies to you as well," Skylar pointed out. "You have clout. You're the police chief."

"I'm also little Viv, Jimi's granddaughter. And I'm massively pregnant, which undermines my status as a kickass chick."

"Checking out the fancy hotel…" Following up on the lead from Jillian was worth the trip. "I'll give it a shot."

"Thanks so much."

Skylar noted the time—3:42. She didn't want to waste another minute. Turning her attention back to Dagmar and Pierce, she asked, "Could up drive me to the Pierpoint?"

"Sure," Dagmar said. "But why?"

"I'm looking for Rogers's son and might need someone to identify him. Would you recognize him, Pierce?"

"I believe so."

The buxom, wild-haired librarian linked her arm with Pierce's and beamed a smile down at him. "We're in."

THE PIERPOINT HOTEL and Spa in Astoria thrust into the harbor on its own pier, close enough to the monster bridge that Skylar had to tilt her head back to see the high arch. The lines of the hotel were sleek and modern. The entrance combined transparent plexiglass walls with an outdoor display of native species of the Pacific Northwest, including sea otters and sea lions who greeted the guests with growls and barks.

"Love the otters," Dagmar said after she parked her battered station wagon and moved to the railing that enclosed the display. "The rest of this isn't my cup of chai. I prefer something that's natural and wild."

"Like me," Pierce said.

"Still," Dagmar continued, "the patrons are willing to pay exorbitant sums to stay here and get massaged."

"And I'm happy to do it for free, luv." Pierce turned to Skylar when they gathered outside the station wagon. "What's the plan?"

She explained. "The woman at the front desk told Chief Kim that Bradley wasn't registered here. Then she refused to take steps to search for him."

"Got it," Dagmar said. "Are we going to beat the truth out of her? Smack her around? Get out the rubber hoses? I always carry pepper spray in my purse. A special formula that Pierce makes for me."

"You're here as backup," Skylar said. "Don't say or do anything unless you see Bradley walking around in the lobby."

The next step in her plan depended on whether or not they found a room number for Bradley. Smoothing the lapels of her jacket, she stalked across the marble floor of the lobby to the front desk made of frosted glass and etched with the sights of Astoria, including the bridge, the historic column atop the hill, a row of pines and seagoing sailing vessels.

The woman standing behind the desk wore a salmon-colored uniform jacket with a gold-plated name tag: Leah Fairchild.

Skylar stormed the desk and thrust her badge into Leah's smug face. She introduced herself loudly enough for others in the area to overhear. "Special Agent Skylar Gambel of the FBI. I have questions for you regarding the current serial killings."

"Hush." Leah placed her index finger across her lips as if talking to a toddler at nappy time. "We don't want you frightening the customers, do we?"

"They should be scared." Skylar made eye contact with a few well-dressed guests of the hotel. "The situation is dangerous, dire, fraught."

Leah scowled. "What do you want from me, Special Agent?"

"Earlier today, APD Chief Kim asked if Bradley Rogers was staying here."

"He's not registered here. That's all I'll tell you."

"You can do more," Skylar said.

"How about a warrant? Why are you bothering me?" Leah's voice got shrill. "What's your problem, lady?

Skylar calmly explained, "I want to look at your records for the past week. Then, I would like to show Bradley's photo to your staff and interview them. I advise you to cooperate."

"Are you threatening me?"

"Certainly not." Skylar held her impatience in check. "I will obtain search warrants and go through all proper procedures."

"That's better," Leah said.

"May I remind you that time is of the essence. The Shadowkeeper has already killed twice. Other lives may be at stake."

Pierce stepped up beside her at the counter. "May I make a suggestion?"

Skylar turned to him, hoping he had an answer for this largely unproductive conversation. "Go ahead."

"Back in high school, Bradley sometimes used the surname of his rich Texan stepfather. Knox."

Skylar glared across the counter at Leah. "Do you have someone named Knox registered?"

"I do," Leah admitted grudgingly. "J. B. Knox in room 460."

On her phone, Skylar pulled up a recent photo of Joseph Bradley Rogers and showed it to Leah. "Is this Knox?"

She nodded. "Is he the killer?"

"Thanks so much for your cooperation," Skylar said.

She pivoted and went toward the elevator. In moments, they stood outside his door, ready to knock. They'd found him, at last.

THE LONG DAY faded into dusk, and the Sand Bar filled with people who had come to talk about the murder of Lucille Dixon, aka the songbird. Jake's private conversation with Xander was cut short again and again by mourners who wanted to hear her favorite tune or offer condolences. The guitarist's comments touched lightly on evidence and heavily on emotion. He missed her. His heart was shattered. His future, dim.

At Jake's urging, Xander focused on those who might have wanted to do her harm. Lucille had known several men but only had problems with a few. A couple of guys cheated on her, but there wasn't a special enemy. People liked her. Xander gestured to the growing crowd. "See them. They had a connection that went deeper than just liking her music."

"Tell me about grudges," Jake said. "Bitter rivals. Someone looking for revenge."

"Everybody loved her." Xander dabbed at the corner of his soulful brown eyes. He sang mostly folk songs and looked like the part with long, glossy black hair and thick stubble. "Lucille was something else. Stomping around in her brave red boots and making people grin. She was one of a kind."

A young woman with a long braid poked her nose into their talk. "Excuse me, Xander, would you play 'Leavin' on a Jet Plane'? I loved the way Lucille sang that tune."

Jake waved her off. "We're talking, ma'am."

"Just one song. Please."

Jake stood, took the guitar and motioned for Xander to follow him to the backstage area beyond the bathrooms. A small storage room, packed with broken tables and cardboard boxes, had been turned into a dressing room for the musical performers. Though it was aboveground, the area smelled like a musty basement. Two makeup mirrors encircled by lights hung over a scarred wooden table where bits of makeup, used tissue and hand lotion were scattered. Four rickety chairs waited at the table. Jake closed the door and directed Lucille's boyfriend to sit.

"In the past week or so," Jake said, "did you notice anything unusual about Lucille?"

"Her Texas accent got thicker. Lots of y'all and howdy and such."

"I don't understand. Why is that important?"

Xander tapped on the side of his head as though jump-starting his brain. "When she was around other people from Texas, she picked it up."

"Who was she with?" Jake thought of Bradley who'd spent half his life in Texas and had a Houston address, but he didn't want to lead Xander to a false memory. "Give me a name."

"Sorry. I can't think of a particular person."

Jake switched to a new direction. "Did she tell you why she hopped into her little red Kia and drove to the North Head Lighthouse last night? Did she have a friend who lived there? Was she meeting someone?"

"It was an appointment," he said.

Now they were getting somewhere. "Odd location for a meeting."

"Lucille wrote a ballad about Cape Disappointment and broken dreams." His eyes misted, and he blinked to keep the tears from falling. "Gentle melody. Beautiful lyrics. She wanted to evoke loneliness and the hope for a brighter horizon. The top of the lighthouse seemed like a good place to take promo photos."

"In the dark?"

"The photographer had some kind of special lens that gave sharp focus, even at night in the fog. They planned to climb to the beacon and take the pictures there."

In one quick statement, so much was explained. Lucille went to the lighthouse after dark when it was closed to the general public. And she climbed to the upper level for the dramatic photo, which meant there was no need for the killer to drag her up the winding staircase. Only one question, the most important one, remained. "Who was the photographer?"

"I don't know. She said he wanted to be anonymous."

Jake's gut clenched. He didn't want to think it was Quilling, but the prior evidence had pointed toward him. Quilling had taken photos of Phoebe. Had he applied the same method to get close to Lucille? His vehicle had been caught by traffic cams on the bridge, proof that his battered old Toyota had made the round trip to Cape Disappointment. Even if Delilah had been in the car, Quilling could have been the driver. "Was it someone local?"

"I didn't recognize him."

"You saw him?" Pulling information from Xander was like peeling layers from an onion. "Describe him."

"Brown hair. Pale skin. A fussy dresser, the kind of guy who wants starch in his shirt and a crease in his jeans."

That didn't sound like Quilling. "Did he wear glasses?"

"Nope, and I couldn't see his eye color from across the room."

"What else?"

"Not too husky. He was tall." Xander chuckled. "Made himself look even taller by wearing cowboy boots."

So far, Jake and Skylar had only discovered one suspect who dressed like a Texan—the elusive Bradley Rogers. He hoped Skylar had tracked him down at the Pierpoint, and they could take him into custody. Maybe tonight there would be no murder.

He wrapped up his interview with Xander with a few more basic questions and advice for him to call or text if he remembered anything more. Jake released the guitarist at the same time Skylar came into the tiny backstage room. The fresh citrus scent of her shampoo cut through the dismal stink. The makeup lights brightened.

She closed the door and turned toward him. "I found Bradley. He used the surname of his stepfather in Texas. Registered at the Pierpoint as J. B. Knox."

"A fake name?"

"Actually, no. He has an innocent excuse because his credit card is in the Knox name, which he must have used when he lived in Texas."

"A spare identity," he said. "Handy."

"Anyway, we went to his room and convinced the snobby front desk woman to let us in. His bed was made, his suitcase gone, and there was no sign of him."

"Had he checked out?"

"Not yet." She shook her head, and her dark curls bounced around her shoulders. Her cheeks were rosy from being outdoors in the wind. "I left a voicemail for Bradley on the phone number Delilah gave me. Asking him to call me. As if? Also, a text. I wish there was something else we could do to find him."

"You could always eat." Jake held up a doggie bag from the restaurant. "Your burger."

"Thoughtful." She snatched it from him, extracted a limp, soggy French fry and dropped it back into the sack. Belated burgers and fries didn't make good leftovers. "I talked to Crawford, and he has information from the autopsy. Wants us to meet him and Jimi at the APD."

Jillian burst through the door. "Skylar, you have to come with me. Right now. Right this minute. He's here."

"Bradley Rogers?"

"He's here," she said breathlessly. "Brought a huge bouquet of flowers in remembrance of Lucille."

Jake dashed down the corridor, passed the bathrooms and charged into the Sand Bar, which was now almost full.

A giant display of yellow roses stood on the bar like a shrine to Lucille Dixon.

Chapter Twenty

Skylar read the printed ribbon draped across the flower basket: *In Memory of Lucille Dixon, Our Yellow Rose from Texas*.

The customers and crew surged around the bar. Some wept. Others raised their craft beer bottles in a toast. When a woman sang an alto version of "Your Cheatin' Heart," others joined in.

Skylar searched their faces, looking for a brown-haired man in his late twenties who matched the photos she had of Bradley. She recognized Ty McKenna with his short, black hair and a hipster-style vest decorated with a pewter watch chain. Tabitha, the goth girl from the *Sun* office, was also there. The three short blond bloggers in their pink-on-pink outfits tried to maintain funereal composure without giggling.

From his taller vantage point, Jake also scanned the crowd that had swelled to over fifty, which she supposed was a lot for early evening. Lucille Dixon must have been well-liked and well-known—a profile that also applied to Phoebe Conway.

If the Shadowkeeper targeted this type of woman, Skylar wondered about his motivation. Lucille and Phoebe might have both embarrassed him in a personal encounter. Or he might have been magnetically drawn to these attractive women. He'd appealed to their vanity to lure them into a dangerous situation. Then he'd attacked. In anger. Or revenge. Or seeking notoriety.

Jillian waved frantically, and Skylar rushed to where she was standing near the exit. Jake was right behind her. Jillian pulled them out the door and pointed into the depths of the jam-packed parking lot. "Bradley is over there. Driving away in a silver BMW. I wrote down the license number."

Skylar took the scrap of paper torn from the waitress's order pad and squinted toward the parking lot exit in time to see the Bimmer merge into traffic. If they hoped to catch him, they needed to move fast.

Jake dashed toward the Explorer only to find it penned in by other cars. With no time to maneuver, he looked for another way out. As if on cue, Dagmar's station wagon chugged to a stop beside them.

"Need a lift?" Dagmar asked.

Skylar watched an array of emotions flicker behind Jake's eyes. He didn't want his cousin involved in the investigation because of the danger. But her offer was the quickest solution to their problem. He desperately wanted to catch up with Bradley, but calling on Dagmar freaked him out. She was the very definition of a loose cannon.

Skylar took charge. Turning to Jillian, she snapped, "Get the area around Jake's Explorer cleared. We'll pick it up later." She shoved him toward the open rear door of Dagmar's car. "Get in." To Dagmar, she said, "Follow that Bimmer."

With a wild grin, Dagmar punched the accelerator, and they took off. "Yeehaw!"

In the passenger seat beside her, Pierce leaned forward as far as his seat belt would allow and fixated on the distant view through the windshield. "Stay on the riverfront road until the traffic clears. Then we'll have a better visual on the silver car."

Skylar was surprised by his sharp analysis. "I thought you didn't like driving."

"Doesn't mean I can't find my way around," he said. "On my bicycle, I think ahead so I can access the most efficient routes. It's all about math and percentages. Bradley is *not* headed to the Pierpoint, which is north of our location. Most of the local businesses are in the opposite direction. Unless he's planning to stop in town, I figure the odds are that he's headed toward the main thoroughfare. Highway 101."

And the highway meant they'd have to cross the bridge. It took a moment for her to remember that the towering Astoria-Megler Bridge was in the rearview mirror. Ahead was the bridge across Youngs Bay that she'd already managed to cross twice without a massive phobic reaction. Only a bit of nausea. And hyperventilation. Racing pulse and—

Jake tapped her arm. "Are we sure that's Bradley's car?"

"He signed in at the hotel with that make and model." Skylar took the note from Jillian out of her pocket and compared it with her data from the Pierpoint. "The license plates match. I already checked with the rental place at the Portland airport."

"When did he pick up the Bimmer?"

"Ten days ago."

He slid across the back seat until he was right beside her. The warmth of his body soothed her momentary panic about the approaching bridge, and she wondered if he had also been concerned about her phobia. With no tugboat in sight, he might be offering himself as a security blanket. But when she glanced up and read his expression, she could see that he'd wanted to be near her for a less drastic reason: he wanted to be close. She understood. After a few hours apart, she was glad to reciprocate.

She snuggled against him but didn't attempt to wrap her arm around his shoulders—a move that Dagmar or Pierce would notice. Though not embracing, their upper bodies touched, and she matched the length of her thigh with his longer, more muscular leg.

For him to get close like this meant he wasn't wearing his

seat belt. Breaking the rules, but she didn't mind. Her hand glided from his knee to his upper thigh.

He rested his hand atop hers. "Bradley has been in town for ten days."

"Uh-huh."

"And never visited his dad. Do you believe that?"

Skylar mumbled her assent. Forcing herself to be coherent, she tossed out another piece of data. "He used the Knox credit card for the rental car."

"Hey, you two." Dagmar darted her station wagon through traffic. On the bridge, she wouldn't be able to change lanes. "He's crossing Youngs Bay, headed for Warrenton."

Skylar stared into Jake's blue, blue eyes. And she sang, "Rolling, rolling, rolling on the river."

Though it didn't make sense, he joined in on the "Proud Mary" chorus. Of course, Pierce sang harmony.

She felt the jolt as the tires bounced onto the paved surface of the two-lane bridge. Not a long drive. Less than a mile. Completely distracted by the rhythmic beat and the intoxicating nearness of Jake's body, she experienced a very mild phobic reaction. She had this. She was under control. *What could go wrong?*

"Damn it!" Dagmar yelled as she slowed drastically. The traffic ahead of them was a stream of red brake lights. "The bridge is lifting."

"What do you mean?" Skylar demanded.

Pierce explained. "Midway across the bridge is a vertical lift section that can be raised to accommodate tall ships and sailboats. There's nothing we can do but wait."

Stuck on the bridge. A nightmare scenario. She gripped Jake's hand, clinging to him. In her rational mind, she knew nothing terrible would strike them down. No trolls or kraken lived beneath the bridge.

But her panic wasn't rational. Her pulse raced. Her throat closed. She gasped for breath.

Dagmar rolled to a complete stop.

Traffic going in the opposite direction passed them, one car at a time. The last rays of sunlight before dusk glinted off the silver BMW as it drove toward them.

Skylar thrust her arm between the two front seats and pointed. "It's him."

Bradley had doubled back from the Warrenton side and was returning to Astoria. He'd returned quickly enough to get past the vertical lift. As his car came closer, she imagined she could see him peering through the windshield, laughing at them.

Without really being aware of her actions, Skylar realized her hand was on the butt of her Glock, ready to draw and shoot. Not a smart move. Not safe at all. She ordered herself to stand down.

Dagmar lacked her self-control. There was a break in the oncoming traffic after Bradley's car, and she flipped her station wagon into Drive. With aggressive maneuvering, she managed to make a U-turn in the middle of the bridge. She headed to Astoria, two cars back from the BMW.

Talk about breaking the rules! Dagmar's actions would have earned her a half-dozen traffic citations if the entire APD hadn't been preoccupied with chasing the Shadow-keeper. She would have been in big trouble. And yet, she'd pulled it off.

Skylar bounced on the seat, cheering Dagmar on. She could tell that neither Jake nor Pierce were thrilled, but she didn't give a damn. All that mattered was catching up to Bradley.

Her bridge panic morphed into a manic phase. Something she'd never experienced before. A state of euphoria. An extreme grin stretched her mouth. Her heartbeat whirred like a hummingbird inside her rib cage.

Dagmar was forced to stop at the light at the end of the bridge. The Bimmer, two cars ahead, made it through and turned right into the hills rising above the marina and the waterfront shops. Once again, Bradley Rogers, aka Knox, was getting away.

Her spirits crashed, and she slumped back against the seat. Too embarrassed to gaze directly at Jake, she focused on her fingers as they twisted into a knot on her lap. "Sorry. I got carried away."

"It's okay." He leaned close and whispered, "I like this better than the last time we crossed a bridge."

"I almost pulled my gun."

"But you didn't." He lightly kissed her cheek. "Sit up so you can watch for Bradley's car along the street."

They made a search, following a grid set out by Pierce, and finally decided they'd lost him. Dagmar drove them back to the Sand Bar where Jake's Explorer had been extricated from the clogged parking lot. From there, they proceeded to the APD where they would meet with Crawford, Jimi and Chief Vivianne.

"I'm hungry," she said.

"Not interested in the cold cheeseburger?"

"I've got a fairly simple appetite, but there are some things I won't touch. Soggy fries and cold burgers drenched in mustard and pickle chips are inedible."

The daylight had rapidly faded into foggy darkness. She could feel the danger closing in. When her phone made the subtle ping announcing the arrival of a new text, she groaned. The message was probably from him.

She read:

Tick tock. Time running out, Skylar. The game is between you and me. Poker players. All in, betting all the marbles.

Warning: I never lose. Tonight, I give the bloggers something to write their columns about. The Shadowkeeper

The mention of bloggers was a warning. Thinking of the three blond influencers she'd just seen in the Sand Bar, Skylar called Chief Kim and asked her to have someone warn them and advise them not to go out tonight.

Chapter Twenty-One

The direct focus of the Shadowkeeper's latest text was Skylar, which worried Jake a lot. Phrases like *the game is between you and me* and *I never lose* made his message clear. The Shadowkeeper had challenged her to a showdown and had no intention of failing.

Driving to the APD, Jake looked over at her in the passenger seat and said, "That text is meant to be personal."

"Well, yeah. It's addressed to me and came through on my phone."

"It's not about your job. It's about you. The Shadowkeeper wants you for his next victim." In their talk about victimology, they'd sketched the rough outlines of a profile. Both Phoebe and Lucille were young and beautiful—local celebrities who worked in visible professions. People recognized them and talked about them. "You have a lot in common with the victims."

"Not really," she said. "I'm not a hometown gal."

"Lucille came from Texas. Phoebe, too. She grew up in Houston."

"Exactly." She dropped her index finger on the console to make her point. "The Texas connection is one of the reasons we suspect Bradley. His mom took him there after they were threatened by the Lightkeeper. She married Knox the rancher who, for all practical purposes, became Bradley's stepfather."

He heard a pensive note in her voice and knew her mind had wandered. "What else?"

"I was thinking about that rusted swing set in the yard beside Rogers's house. He could have trashed it long ago, but he keeps it there as if he's expecting to look out the window and see his son going down the slide. And he has a Little League photo of young Bradley in his office. I think he loves his son."

Jake had sensed the same thing. "Maybe Bradley feels the same way about his dad, and that's why he came back to Astoria."

"To show his love by killing young women?" She shook her head. "I took my thinking in a different direction, concentrating on the stepfather. Based on inference and hearsay without a shred of tangible evidence, I'm guessing that the gun-toting Knox abused Bradley. Physically and verbally. His mother's second husband seems like somebody who'd tell a kid that he had to kick butt to prove he was a man. And some women like men who take charge."

He agreed with all she'd said. "As you pointed out, we have no proof. Nothing to go on."

"And no time to go deep." She looked at her watch again. "If we could interview Bradley or have a team from the Behavioral Analysis Unit interview him, we could make a case."

Again, he agreed, but he wouldn't let her drag him off track. "We were talking about why the Shadowkeeper threw down that challenge. Like you, both of the victims were headstrong, intelligent and talented. Phoebe was a journalist. Lucille was a singer."

"And what's my talent?"

He shot her a glance. "My guess is martial arts."

"You've never seen me in action."

"They don't hand out brown belts to just anybody." He'd looked up her background information on the internet and discovered that she was something of a legend in San Francisco martial arts tournaments. "Do I need to track down some-body at your dojo to find out how many awards you've won?"

"I do okay," she said.

"Most important, both of our victims were competitive, driven to succeed. Like you. The Shadowkeeper used their ambition to lure them into danger."

Skylar couldn't deny that similarity. She'd told him how hard she worked to earn her position as a special agent. She'd dedicated herself to investigating and solving crimes, start-ing with the apprehension of the Shadowkeeper. "You might be onto something," she admitted. "If he was going to hook me into doing something stupid, he'd appeal to my need to apprehend him."

He imagined a text the Shadow might send. "He'd start with something about how you're a brilliant investigator and deserve to make this arrest. Playing to your ambition. Then he'd invite you to a dark, lonely lighthouse."

"We can use his challenge to set a trap."

This was the second time she'd suggested something like this, and he still wasn't interested in risking her life. He knew exactly what he intended to do. From now on, he'd be with her all day and all night. She'd never admit to needing a pro-tector, but she did. "We've got to be hyperaware. Watch for him to make the first move."

"And find him tonight. Right now. Before he kills again."

At APD command central, Jake delivered a point-by-point briefing on their findings. They would continue to monitor Rogers the editor, Delilah the magenta-haired girlfriend, Quilling and Ty McKenna, but they focused on Bradley Rog-ers as their primary suspect.

Crawford and Jimi Kim had researched and interrogated the two suspects from twenty years ago and their families. Though disappointed, the two investigators agreed that neither of these two bad guys warranted further surveillance. In spite of prior involvement in petty crimes and misdemeanors, these men and their families lived unremarkable lives and had valid alibis.

Chief Vivienne Kim waddled to the front of the room and took a position with her pregnant belly obscuring the lower frames of a wide-screen feed set up by the FBI techs. "We have ten camera positions at possible locations. Officers are standing by, ready to respond."

"Impressive," Skylar said. She filled a plate with Nana's homemade Italian dinner, featuring lasagna, pizza, caprese, bowls of Caesar salad and Girl Scout cookies. "Who do you have stationed near the miniature golf course?"

"Since you and Jake seem to think the seventh hole with the lighthouse replica is our next target, I put our best team on it. Dot and Dub."

Jake studied the camera feed, watching as a foursome of young teens lined up their shots. The surveillance screens were set to mute, but reading the giggles and teasing from the golfers wasn't difficult. The limited range of vision showed several people on the course, which featured mastheads, bridges, a shark with an open mouth and an octopus with arms that blocked the path of the ball to the hole. "Too many witnesses," he said. "When does it close?"

"Eleven o'clock on a weeknight. By midnight, everybody should be gone."

Skylar checked her wristwatch, a timekeeping gesture he was beginning to find annoying. "It's 8:47," she said. "Gets dark early here. Something to do with the fog?"

"Actually," Jimi said wryly. "It's because the sun goes down."

Jake never knew when to take the wiry old gent seriously. Jimi's enigmatic interrogation technique had fascinated him since he was a kid spying on the local police. After Jimi asked his series of questions, the person being interrogated was often too confused to do anything but confess. Jake trusted the former chief of police completely. "Tell us what you learned from the autopsy."

"Both victims were administered a drug by syringe. The final toxicology report is pending, and Dr. Kinski doesn't like to make guesses. But her initial analysis indicates the presence of ketamine and points to a fast-acting anesthetic." To illustrate, he held up his hand with fingers splayed to countdown. "Going backward from one hundred, you will reach ninety-nine, ninety-eight and then be out cold. Contusions indicate that the victims were already handcuffed when drugged. No other signs of premortem injuries."

Crawford added. "He knocked them out, then killed them, then posed them."

"Cause of death?" Jake asked.

Jimi responded, "Asphyxiation. Broken hyoid bones on each victim. Phoebe was garroted with a thin cord which was not found at the crime scene. Lucille was manually strangled before being hung from a noose."

"Were they raped?" Skylar asked.

"Not Phoebe." Jimi pursed his lips and shook his head. "For Lucille, the evidence is pending. She engaged in sexual intercourse shortly before her death, but there were no signs of violence. The act may have been consensual."

"Or she was unconscious." Apparently, that thought disturbed Skylar so much that she set down her fork and stopped eating. "Unable to struggle."

Jimi said, "Traces of semen were left behind. Dr. Kinski will run DNA tests."

Jake remembered his conversation with Xander, Lucille's boyfriend, who told him they were together before she left for Cape Disappointment. The folk singer never mentioned having sex, but Jake hadn't specifically asked. He needed to go back to the Sand Bar for verification from Xander. Also, one of the bartenders hinted that Ty McKenna was known for his grandiose lies and practical jokes—possible indications that his alibi wasn't rock-solid.

Jake listened while Crawford tweaked a few more threads of evidence. The knots on the noose around Lucille's throat were typical of those used in boating. Not much of a lead in a harbor town like Astoria where boats were as common as taxis.

"And Lucille's car has been located," Crawford said. "It went off a cliff near the North Head Lighthouse and crashed on the rocks. As far as we can tell, there was no driver or passengers. Someone must have put it in Neutral and shoved. Forensics will study the waterlogged wreckage, but the chances of extracting any viable evidence are slim to none."

"We need a new plan," Jimi announced. "Skylar and Jake, how can we contribute to your investigation?"

"Find Bradley Rogers, who also uses the last name of Knox," Skylar said. "We put out a BOLO on his silver BMW but haven't gotten any hits."

"We're usually more efficient," Chief Kim said with a scowl. "My people are stretched thin. Some are keeping watch over the likely spots for the Shadowkeeper to strike. Others are staking out suspects."

Jake exhaled a long sigh. He wished they could have activated Quilling. His expertise would be helpful. He turned to Skylar. "Show them the latest text."

She pulled up the message on her phone. "I received this just before we came here."

Crawford read quickly, then looked up with worried eyes. "Is this untraceable?"

"I'll check," Chief Kim, "but I suspect he's using the same process as before. He makes the initial contact using a disposable burner, which is not equipped with GPS or tracking. Then he sends the text, dumps the phone and walks away."

"What happens if we find the discarded phone?"

"It's nothing more than a piece of plastic and wires."

"Not if he left fingerprints," Jimi said. "Not likely, but possible."

"Here's my thought," Jake said. "The Shadowkeeper enjoys outsmarting us. In his messages, he keeps leaving clues and Easter eggs."

Jimi shook his head. "What does this mean? An Easter egg?"

"A reference to something hidden in plain sight. Like on an Easter egg hunt." Jake offered an example. "When the Shadowkeeper sent us to Cape Disappointment, that was a clue. Mentioning a hole-in-one might be an Easter egg pointing to the miniature golf course."

"He likes puzzles," Crawford said. "We should break down all his messages and see what might be significant. I seem to recall that he consistently mentions Phoebe's columns. Do we have copies?"

Chief Kim shuffled through stacks of paperwork from the *Sun,* searching for relevant documents while Crawford and Jimi laid out the various messages from the Shadowkeeper and attempted to decipher his meaning.

In the meantime, Jake and Skylar would return to the Sand Bar to find Xander.

ON A THURSDAY NIGHT, the street outside the police department was relatively quiet, broken only by the occasional cries of gulls, a foghorn and the hiss of tires against pavement.

Skylar squinted through the swirling mist outside the windshield. She took a sip from a container of pomegranate juice from the spread laid out in command central. "I'm glad we're able to follow our instincts. SSA Crawford trusts us. He's still encouraging me to investigate in the field."

"He'd switch directions in a minute if I mentioned your idea to use yourself as bait."

"Nobody likes a tattletale, Jake."

The quiet of the night shattered into a wild cacophony that spilled into the night when they drove close to the Sand Bar. Apparently, the disorganized wake for Lucille Dixon that started with a yellow rose bouquet had escalated into high gear.

Jake parked across the street outside a closed dry cleaner shop to avoid getting trapped in the parking lot again. "Do you think Bradley came back here after he dropped off the flowers?"

"Wouldn't that be a stroke of luck," she said. "When we're done here, we should pay his father a visit. Now that we have proof that Bradley is in Astoria, his dad might be willing to tell us why he returned to his hometown."

"Also, we need to hit the miniature golf course," he reminded her.

A dozen small projects called for their attention, but their priority was to interpret the messages the Shadowkeeper had sent. Skylar hated to imagine his glee, thinking he'd outsmarted them, tossing out clues and laughing when they charged off in the wrong direction.

As soon as she and Jake stepped through the door, she saw that the single display of yellow roses had been augmented by several other floral tributes to Lucille. "Red Roses for a Blue Lady" and "Sunflower" and "Daisies" celebrated her music. Squawks from the stage signaled a country-western band getting ready to perform. Conversations bloomed with memories and then faded into quiet sorrow.

Skylar felt a prickling across her shoulders—a feeling that someone was watching her.

Jillian raced through the bar with a trayful of beer. Pausing on her route through the tables, she spoke to Skylar. "Haven't seen him again."

"If you do…"

"I'll let you know." She pivoted back toward the table she

was serving and informed them that if they wanted mixed drinks or wine, they needed to go to the bar.

Jake tagged Xander and pulled him aside. "Thought you were scheduled to sing tonight."

"It's too loud and too crazy for my kind of music," he said. "I just want to go home and sit with my memories of Lucille."

Clearly, this wasn't the most sensitive time to pose uncomfortable questions. Still, Jake pushed forward. "Last night before Lucille left for her photo session, did you make love to her?"

"I did." Xander's soulful brown eyes shone with tears. A single droplet slipped down his cheek into the thick stubble that outlined his high cheekbones. "I'll miss her."

Unable to gaze directly at his pain, Skylar looked away. Again, she sensed someone watching. She looked toward the flowers, then to the black-clad mourners mingling with brightly dressed drinkers in Hawaiian shirts. People were laughing. And crying. And cursing. The place was a madhouse. On the stage, the standing cymbals fell to the floor with a discordant crash. When she turned toward the noise, she saw him.

They had never met in person, but the tall man with narrow shoulders resembled the photos she'd seen of Bradley Rogers. Nicely dressed and well-groomed with a light trace of stubble on his chin. His pleasant, unremarkable features and calm attitude allowed him to fade into the crowd. He didn't look like a serial killer. *Neither did Ted Bundy.* She studied him more closely, trying to decide if she was wrong.

His dark-eyed gaze latched on to hers and held her captive. He was the person who had been watching. Her instincts screamed in warning. He meant to do her harm. Cruelty brewed in his gut. Rage and hatred rolled off him in waves.

Even more terrifying was his smile. He was enjoying himself, smirking and licking his upper lip as though savoring a rare rib-eye steak dripping with juice. Casually, he raised his hand and pointed directly at her.

"Jake," she said as she grasped his arm. "Come with me. Now."

"Wait." He was in the middle of his own conversation. "You've got to hear this."

She refused to allow herself to be distracted. Picking her way through the crowd, she moved across the floor. A surge of line dancers arranged themselves in front of her, making it impossible to see Bradley. While she searched, Jake followed. He had Ty McKenna in tow. Finally, they came to a stop.

"Tell her, McKenna."

"Fine," he snapped. "Phoebe wasn't as important as she thought. You asked me about her columns. And I informed you that she never had a column. She wasn't good enough."

Skylar had lost track of Bradley in the crowd. He was escaping from her again. Desperately, she shoved her way to the corner where he'd been standing. *Gone!*

"Did you hear that?" Jake asked. "Phoebe had a byline that she used for articles like *The Goonies* story and the piece she did on Lucille Dixon. But no column."

Frustrated, she whipped around to face him. "So what?"

"It's the Easter egg, Skylar. He mentions the column in almost every message."

"Something hiding in plain sight."

"The Astoria Column," Jake said in his tour-guide voice, "was dedicated in 1926 by the Astors and the people who ran the Great Northern Railway. It stands on Coxcomb Hill overlooking the mouth of the Columbia. The tower is one hundred twenty-five feet high, and it looks like…the grandest lighthouse on the coast."

The site of the next murder.

Chapter Twenty-Two

Back in the Explorer, Skylar put through a call to SSA Crawford while Jake contacted Chief Kim using his two-way radio earbud. The Astoria Column was less than ten minutes away from the Sand Bar, using a shortcut Jake had learned years ago when he was a tour guide. The gates into the five-acre park surrounding the monument weren't locked until ten. A few sightseers might still be parked there, watching the hourly display when the spotlights against the column cycled through every shade in the rainbow.

"Contact the park service and tell the rangers to stand down," he said to Chief Kim. "Skylar and I will be at the scene in a couple of minutes, making a final approach on foot. Other officers should be ready for backup if we need assistance. Tell them not to move until you give the word."

"Do you think he's there right now?"

"If he is, I don't want him to escape."

"I'll coordinate timing with the others," Chief Kim said. "The last thing I want is a bunch of armed, excitable cops blundering around without direction."

"Copy that. I'll be in touch."

Relying on memory, Jake took a narrow backroad to a little-used gate where he parked. Completely hidden by forest on the lower slope of Coxcomb Hill, he peered through the fog to glimpse the spectacular structure with the history of the Columbia River depicted in carved, painted scenes encircling the column. He glanced toward Skylar, who leaned so far forward that her nose almost touched the windshield. "Can you see it?"

"It's mostly hidden by the trees," she said, "but impressive, nonetheless. Why was it built?"

"As a tribute to the people of the Northwest. The artwork starts after the first contact with Chinook and Clatsop tribes and extends to the opening of the railroad. My Norwegian great-great-grandpa Gunderson on my mom's side could trace his roots to the early days. Jimi Kim's family was here earlier than that. They came as fishermen from the part of Asia now known as South Korea." And he didn't need to be giving her a history lesson. Not while they were so close to catching the Shadowkeeper. "I'll turn off the light over the dashboard so nobody will notice when we get out of the Explorer."

"He's not here," she said firmly. "I saw Bradley at the Sand Bar. He vanished before I could talk to him."

"Why didn't you say anything?"

"I had to talk to Crawford, and I wasn't totally sure what was happening. He just vanished. The place was crowded, chaotic and too loud to even think. But I really think it was him. He stared at me. His eyes were like tractor beams. Then he cocked and pointed his index finger."

"Like aiming a gun?" Jake hated the threat. He wished he could take her back to the Captain's Cove where she'd be safe. "Maybe we should wait for backup."

"The two of us should be able to handle one creepy, narcissistic, psychopathic serial killer."

He knew she intended to make a joke, but he wasn't laughing. "Not funny."

"I'd rather maintain the element of surprise."

"You're right." But the Shadowkeeper had already killed

twice. He didn't want Skylar to be the next trophy on his mantel. If she knew how much he feared for her safety and how much she meant to him, she'd be furious. She'd tell him in no uncertain terms how qualified she was to take care of herself with her brown belt in karate and top ranking as a sharpshooter.

"By the way," she said, "Crawford was impressed with your insight about the difference between a newspaper column and the Astoria Column."

He turned off the overhead light and eased open the car door. "Stick close to me. The entrance is on the opposite side."

"Are rangers manning the building?"

"Right now, nobody is on-site. The gift shop is closed. The front gate will be locked at ten, about a half hour from now." He led the way from the trees to their first unobstructed view of the one-hundred-twenty-five-foot-tall column. "It's almost a hundred years old. When they first erected it, the Astoria Column was supposed to rival the Eiffel Tower. Unfortunately, they didn't consider the effects of constant wind and rain against the artistic carvings. The column has undergone several repairs and renovations, including a seismic upgrade."

She paused beside him. "It's a good thing you're cute."

"Why is that?"

"In spite of your height, muscles and background in the US Marines, you're kind of a history nerd."

"Guilty." Now was probably not the best time to brag about his comic book collection. He unholstered his Beretta and crossed the mowed grass surrounding the concrete patio and walkway outside the column. In the parking lot on the opposite side of the structure, he saw only one vehicle. A sporty blue Toyota SUV. Not the silver Bimmer driven by Bradley.

"I hope we're wrong," she whispered. "I don't want to find another victim."

"From the number of times he mentioned 'columns,' it's

obvious that he planned to use this place from the start. He might also have preselected his victims. We know he stalked Phoebe."

"Did he?" she asked. "Joe Rogers's car was parked outside her apartment, but we have no evidence against Bradley. And we don't know why Delilah's hair was found in Quilling's car."

They reached the edge of the concrete patio, complete with walkway and benches. Nothing seemed unusual or out of place. He led her to the entrance of a small building at the base of the column. A numerical keypad beside the door unlocked the monument. Years ago, he had the right combination to do an open-sesame, but when he tried the series of six digits, nothing happened. "I'll get the code from Chief Kim."

With her back to him and her Glock 19 held at the ready, she stayed alert and scanned the grounds. "I don't see the driver of the SUV. Is there anywhere else a tourist might go?"

"Not that I know."

Chief Kim got back to him quickly, and he punched in the code. The door opened, and overhead lights came on automatically. Inside, he glanced at the display cases, sepia photographs from the early 1900s and historical artifacts. His attention was immediately drawn to the inner area where a wrought iron spiral staircase rose to the upper observation deck that encircled the cupola.

Jake recognized the third victim. Chief Kim was supposed to reach out to her but must have been too late. This young, blond woman was one of those who blogged about true crime, and her name was…something Shakespearean, like her sister Juliet. He snapped his fingers. "Portia. Her name is Portia. A high school senior."

Portia was arranged in a pose similar to the photos he'd seen of the crime scene at Cape Meares. With her long, denim-clad legs tucked under her, she sat on the third step from the floor. A forest green bandanna blindfolded her eyes and pulled her curly hair back behind her ears. Silver duct tape covered her mouth. Zip ties fastened her wrists to the railing on the staircase.

Skylar felt for a pulse. Excited, she said, "She's still breathing."

Immediately, he alerted Chief Kim. "Call an ambulance. We found an unconscious woman inside the column."

With the ambulance on the way, he took out his Leatherman pocketknife and sliced through the zip ties. Portia's limp body fell into Skylar's arms. Together, they lowered her to the floor. When Skylar tore the tape from her mouth, they heard the welcome sound of a gasp. But her eyelids remained closed. Portia was alive but unconscious.

Cradling the young woman in her arms, Skylar gently unwound a long knitted scarf from around her throat. All the while, she spoke softly and offered reassurances. When the scarf was removed, Portia's neck showed signs of bruising.

A jolt of anger went through Jake. The Shadowkeeper had attacked this young woman, a high schooler. Why? And why had he stopped choking her before she was dead?

"Ask her who did this. Did she see him?" He was anxious to gather as much information as possible. Based on the tox screen from the ME, the Shadowkeeper used a ketamine-based anesthetic, fast-acting and available from many sources including thrill-seekers and veterinarians. A small dose shouldn't be life-threatening, but he didn't know for sure. "Ask her."

Skylar shot him an annoyed glance and continued her one-sided conversation. "Portia, can you tell me what happened? Is that your sporty blue SUV parked in front?"

Portia gave no response.

It occurred to Jake that the Shadowkeeper might still be in this building. There weren't many places to hide in the concrete tower, but he needed to check the place out. With his Beretta in hand, he circled the lower two floors, entering every closet, bathroom and office. In the small women's bathroom on the second floor, he found splatters of water and muddy footprints. The Shadowkeeper might have hidden in here with Portia, waiting for the rangers to lock the column for the night.

When he returned to the central area where Skylar was still comforting the victim, Jake looked up at the spiral staircase. From his tour guide days, he knew there were one hundred and sixty-four steps. Not a trek he wanted to make unless he had to.

As the distant squeal of the ambulance grew louder, Skylar waved him over. She held up a postcard with the column on the front and said, "I found this tucked into Portia's bra."

He read the note written on the back:

Hi Skye. Thought I'd give you a break with this one. Pretty little Portia looked lonely. Do you ever feel that way? All alone without a crew or a partner or a husband? It's your curse.

You're next, Special Agent. When you die, wait for me. The Shadowkeeper

The threat couldn't have been more direct or personal. No way would Jake leave her alone until the Shadowkeeper was behind bars.

Chapter Twenty-Three

At 3:23 a.m., Skylar dragged her feet up the sidewalk and across the veranda at the Captain's Cove. Jake had insisted on seeing her home after a long night at the hospital with Portia's family and then at APD command central. They worked with SSA Crawford and Jimi Kim to dissect and analyze evidence while keeping tabs on the surveillance cameras placed throughout the area. *A long night.*

Jake waited patiently for her to unlock the front door to the B&B. Then he followed her inside. Before she could thank him and send him on his way, he strode across the entryway to the carved oak staircase. "I'm coming up to your room," he said.

Ever since he'd read the Shadowkeeper's threat, he'd been extra attentive. Several times, she'd caught him staring at her when he thought she didn't notice. And he'd constantly patrolled up and down the hallways, checking windows and doors. Though she'd told him that she wasn't a delicate little buttercup and could take care of herself, Skylar had to admit she liked his attentions. His gentle touches on her shoulder, back or arm—as if to remind himself she was all right—comforted her in a primal way that didn't sync with her feminist attitude but felt good, damned good.

In her bedroom at the top of the stairs, she unlocked and he entered first with his weapon drawn. Following tried-and-true police procedure, he searched and cleared the bedroom, bathroom and closet. He peered under the bed and assessed the view from the windows to be sure she wasn't in a sniper's line of fire.

"I can see the column from here," he said as he closed the curtains. "Great room."

Too tired to comment, she collapsed onto the pale blue duvet. The firm mattress supported her back and shoulders, encouraging her to grab a few hours of sleep, but as soon as she closed her eyes, her brain awakened.

Their investigation had reached a tipping point. The postcard left on Portia's body had produced a clear thumbprint that matched Bradley Rogers's print from a high school arrest. Until now, he'd been careful not to leave clues, which made her wonder if the card had been planted for them to find. If not, Bradley was the killer. They decided to back off on other suspects and persons-of-interest from twenty years ago. Though their surveillance on lighthouses in the area continued, more effort concentrated on finding Bradley and his BMW.

The quiet in her room told her Jake had completed his search, but she hadn't heard the door close. Peeking through half-opened eyes, she turned her head and saw him standing at the window. He came toward her, lifted her right foot and removed her boot, and then he did the left.

She moaned with pleasure. Relief nearly overwhelmed her. Those boots were comfortable, but she needed to wiggle her toes. "Thanks."

He sat on the bed beside her. His large hand rested on her thigh just above her kneecap. "Is there anything else you want me to help you take off? A jacket? A shirt? A bra?"

Though his tone was playful, her imagination leaped from exhaustion to lust in a single bound. She recalled the moment when she'd impulsively kissed him at Cape Disappointment. *Disappointment? Hah!* There was nothing unsatisfying about the erotic sensation of his rock-hard body pressing against hers.

Using Tucker's tugboat, he had rescued her. Jake had sensed her need to cross the Columbia without a bridge, and he made it happen. He was both a proactive alpha and a sensitive beta. His hand inched higher on her thigh, and she brushed it away before she succumbed to his suggestion, threw away her self-control and begged him to remove every stitch of her clothing.

"Stop," she said in an unconvincing tone.

"In case you're wondering, I'm spending the night in your room."

He didn't ask her permission, and she liked his assertiveness whether she agreed to his plan or not. Acting as her protector made logical sense because the Shadowkeeper had made direct threats against her and preferred to act at night.

Still, she objected. "I don't need a bodyguard."

"We'll see about that." He kicked off his own boots, stood and stretched with his arms over his head. His knuckles brushed the ceiling. From his backpack, he took out a few pieces of electronic equipment that he placed on the table beside his Beretta. "I'm going to scan the room for hidden cameras and bugs. The Shadowkeeper likes stalking, and I want to make sure he's not spying on you."

"Good thinking."

"I have my moments."

She rolled onto her side and propped her chin on her hand to watch him as he swept the bug detector in logical places. He reached high to the crown molding near the ceiling and ducked low to poke beneath the dresser. For a big man, he moved gracefully. His long legs and arms were proportional to his torso and muscular shoulders.

To distract herself from ogling him, she said, "Seems to me that the Shadowkeeper is dissembling, starting with the obvious fact that he didn't kill Portia."

"When she's conscious and able to talk, she might be able to give us an identification."

"I hope so."

He'd told Skylar about the signs of someone hiding in the bathroom at the column, which was a risk. If he'd kept Portia there, he would have needed to keep her drugged for at least three hours. Her level of intoxication would be difficult to balance without triggering an overdose.

Jake must have been thinking along the same lines, because he asked, "Have you heard anything more about her condition?"

"Her parents are with her. She's expected to have a full recovery, but the doctors won't let us question her until morning."

"In another sign of his increasing carelessness," Jake said, "he left a fingerprint."

"Not only the print, but he handed over a sample of his handwriting. His other communications came through untraceable phones and computer links. Even his first note to Phoebe was printed, not written."

"He was equally cautious at the other crime scenes. Our forensic experts haven't turned up enough evidence to identify him. No fibers, hairs or bloodstains."

"On the other hand," she said, "if Bradley is the Shadowkeeper, he didn't bother to hide his credit card in the name of J. B. Knox when he registered at the Pierpoint."

"A sign of inexperience." He shrugged. "Even an intelligent sociopath makes mistakes."

"The FBI cybercrime team in Portland have been tracking his purchases. He hasn't used the card since he checked into the hotel."

"He almost made physical contact with you at the Sand Bar. But then he ran away."

She appreciated this type of analytical discussion almost as much as she enjoyed the opportunity to observe Jake in action. He had turned out to be a great partner when it came to investigating, and she wondered if they'd be compatible in other areas.

"These changes have significance," she said, "but I don't know what it means."

"He's playing a game, and he's getting bored. Murder doesn't give him as much of a thrill as he expected. Like a poker player, he makes the game more interesting and more important by raising the stakes." He replaced his tools in his backpack and approached her bed. "By naming you as his next victim, he escalates to a different level."

"A direct challenge."

"Like a duel." His laser-blue eyes made fiery contact with hers, and they exchanged an unspoken but eloquent message. They were playing for high stakes, indeed. He illustrated by holding out his hand toward her. Resting on his palm were two tiny listening devices that actually did resemble insects. "Gifts from the Shadowkeeper. Should I crush them or keep them?"

She chose another option. "Flush them."

After a quick detour to the bathroom, he returned to her bed and stretched out beside her. His body radiated a pleasant warmth, and she caught a whiff of the outdoorsy scent she'd come to associate with him. "You'll be glad to know that I didn't locate any teeny-tiny cameras."

"Oh, good." She turned toward him. "Then nobody will be able to see me do this."

She glided into his horizontal embrace, tilting her head to snuggle into the curve of his throat. Blazing a trail, she kissed from the dimple on his chin to his jaw and ultimately to his ear where she caught his lobe in her teeth and gently tugged.

He inhaled a ragged breath. "I like that."

She pulled back and gazed into his handsome, chiseled face. "You mentioned something about taking off clothes."

He didn't need a second invitation to unbutton her blouse that had started the day looking fresh and professional. Not anymore. Her clothing was a rumpled mess.

Before he unfastened her bra, she insisted on taking her turn. She unzipped and unbuttoned him. After a slightly frenzied moment, they were both nude from the waist up.

Though she'd imagined being intimate with him, she hadn't planned for what might happen. Or what it meant. Or what sort of relationship they might have. An FBI special agent based in Portland and a police detective from Astoria could certainly be friends. More than that was problematic.

Right now, she'd settle for friends with benefits. And enjoy the ride.

His arm encircled her and pulled her close, matching their naked flesh together and making them as one. Hearts beating in unison. Her breasts rubbed against his chest, and the friction sparked a nascent flame that became a wildfire when she threw her leg over his thighs and wriggled the softest part of her body against the hardest of his.

Passion churned through her and exploded in an incredible kiss. The pressure of their lips alternated between hard and soft, demanding and yielding. His tongue thrust into her mouth and engaged with hers. Teasing. Tasting.

Though she wasn't sexually inexperienced, she'd never felt anything like this before. Amazing sensations quivered across the surface of her skin, and she abandoned herself to these feelings Jake created in her. Like the karate moves called katas that she'd practiced until they were rooted in her memory, she danced in harmony with him. He seemed to anticipate her every pose, and she did the same for him.

Not that they were totally synchronized. There were delightful surprises. She wasn't sure how they got out of their pants and between the sheets but knew their moves didn't follow an elegant choreography. Their passion was directed by feral need and instinct.

Cocooned under the pale blue duvet with the bedside lamp turned low, she gazed into his eyes. Her fingers traced the structure of his face, then slid down to his shoulders and lower. She traced the line of hair from his chest to his groin.

He fondled her breasts, flicking his thumb across her taut nipple and sending shock waves deep into her body.

Between spasms of pleasure, she gasped a single word. "Condom."

He replied, "Yes."

When he rolled away from her to pick his jeans off the floor and find his wallet, she felt bereft, which was ridiculous. She'd only known him for a few days, not long enough for him to become an integral part of her. And yet, she couldn't imagine being apart. A dangerous thought for a woman who had just attained her goal of becoming a special agent.

When he returned to her, she clung tightly to him. "I missed you," she whispered.

"Me, too."

He showed her how much her absence had affected him with an all-consuming kiss. An earthquake so powerful that she felt the aftershocks all the way down to her toes. She had truly come undone. At the same time, she knew exactly what she wanted. When he sheathed himself and penetrated her with hard, strong thrusts, she was driven to climax, again and again and…again. And then…she was complete. Fulfilled. Satisfied.

Lying beside him, looking up at the anchor-patterned wallpaper and the decorative fisherman's net draped in the corner by the window, she smiled. Not just with her lips but with her whole body. Oh yes, this was going to happen again. As soon as possible. Maybe in the morning.

"Tomorrow," she said.

"Yes."

"I really need to take a shower. At least run a comb through my hair or brush my teeth." She couldn't believe she'd let him see her like this. "Actually, I clean up well."

He laced his fingers with hers. "You're perfect."

"But I—"

"Perfect," he said.

She knew it wasn't true. Still, nice to hear.

Chapter Twenty-Four

The next morning at half past seven, Jake wakened to a dull sunrise blanketed in fog. After he stumbled from the bed to the window and opened the curtain, he stood staring and wondering why the weather didn't reflect the glow that radiated from his chest and warmed his entire body.

When he looked at Skylar, still in bed, he saw a reflection of that light in her beautiful smile. For a moment, the clouds outside the window parted, and a ray of sunshine lit the skies. Last night, he'd been more than a friend, more than a bodyguard. He'd taken their partnership to a different level that surprised him and yet felt inevitable.

He was anxious to get started on the day. They needed to find the Shadowkeeper, to end these murders and bring him to justice. Then Jake could move forward to the more important issue of convincing Skylar to fall in love with him.

"Before you start making plans," she said as she rose from the bed, naked and unembarrassed, "you should know that I'm not leaving this room until I wash my hair and take a shower."

"I'll join you."

"Fine by me."

They stood together under steaming jets of water. They kissed, fondled and soaped each other, but there couldn't be a final consummation because he had no more condoms. Picking up a six-pack or a twelve-pack or an entire crate would be the first priority on his to-do list.

When they got to the police station, he planned to change into the fresh clothes he kept in his locker, but Skylar dressed now, selecting another conservative suit and a rose-colored shirt.

He asked, "Do you always wear suits?"

"It's my work uniform. Looks neat, and the jacket is long enough to cover my holster." She scrunched her dark auburn hair to let it air-dry in wavy curls. "Crawford says I dress like a recruitment poster for women in the FBI. Actually, his wife says that. Crawford doesn't notice what I wear."

"Today, I want you to add a bulletproof vest." Thus far, the Shadowkeeper hadn't used a gun, but there was always a first time.

"Fine. I have lightweight flexible body armor that's custom fitted. The color is camo green. Matches my eyes. Very fashionable."

"Is it weird that I'm getting turned on?"

She grinned and lowered her voice to a breathy, sexy level. "The vest has a sheath for my Ka-Bar knife. And extra magazines for my Glock 19."

He cupped his hands over his ears, pretending he couldn't hear. "Stop."

"And then, of course, I have my ankle holster, a pocket switchblade and a razor-edged hairclip for when I fasten my ponytail."

In his opinion, she still needed his protection to watch her six and make sure the Shadowkeeper didn't sneak up behind her. "Let's go."

When they checked in at APD for a briefing from Chief Kim about what happened last night after Portia was rescued, they scarfed down coffee, apple juice, a couple of doughnuts and egg rolls with kimchi and bacon. Last night, the surveillance teams discovered nothing. The officers who staked out suspects' homes saw zero activity. The biggest event was when Officer Dot's nine-year-old daughter got a hole-in-one at the miniature golf course. The Shadowkeeper was AWOL.

Crawford and Jimi Kim showed up with more food and no further leads. The next step for Jake and Skylar would be visiting the hospital to interview Portia. After that, they'd retrace their steps, hoping to find a new direction to search for Bradley.

At 10:45, they heard back from the doctor at Columbia Memorial, a small facility with a heliport and a level-four trauma center. Portia was wide awake and anxious to talk to them. Finally, they might get a definite identification of Bradley as the Shadowkeeper.

On the short drive to the hospital, Jake laid out a strategy. "We need to split up. One of us talks to Portia. The other deals with her parents and friends."

"I'll take Portia," Skylar said. "I'm not good with family."

"Doesn't the FBI train you for interpersonal stuff?"

"We've got classes on interrogation, hostage negotiation, suicide prevention and active shooter situations. Not so much on dealing with an angry parent or pushy friend."

"It's not my favorite thing, either." He shrugged. "Flip a coin. Heads I talk to Portia."

He won the toss. When they got to the hospital, they found her room occupied by a rotating group of parents, sister and friends, including a young man who called himself her fiancé over her sister's objection. Grumbling, Skylar took charge, herding Portia's people into the waiting area with all the warmhearted friendliness of an FBI-trained hostage negotiator.

Jake saw Portia tucked into a bed in a private ICU room, the petite blonde looking vulnerable, afraid and very young. Her vitals were monitored while saline solution dripped into her bloodstream through an IV and a cannula delivered oxygen to her nostrils. Her complexion had paled beneath her tan. She'd covered the dark circles under her eyes with concealer but had done nothing to hide the purplish bruises around her throat and ligature marks on her wrists.

In a hoarse voice, she thanked him for clearing the room. "My parents are so mad. They've told me a million times not to go off by myself. I was stupid, stupid, stupid."

"You made a mistake," he said. "Doesn't mean you're a moron or a failure. Everyone—your family and friends and the people who listen to your podcast—will eventually forget to be angry and will celebrate the fact that you're still alive."

"Thanks, Jake."

"Tell me why you went to the column."

She inhaled a deep breath and the story spilled out. She'd started getting text messages on her phone from someone who said they knew the Shadowkeeper and would give her an exclusive interview. Unfortunately, she couldn't show him the texts because her phone was missing. "He must have taken it."

"What happened when you got there?"

Again, she gave a long-winded explanation which essentially told him that she'd been following directions in the texts that led her to the bathroom on the second floor near the offices which was, apparently, where he held her after the building closed to the public. "At the upstairs bathroom, I pushed the door and went inside. And then…" She went silent.

He prodded. "Did you see him?"

She touched her neck and winced. "I felt a pinprick, like getting stung by a bee. Then I passed out. I don't remember anything else until you and Skylar were standing over me."

Though he reassured her and told her she was brave and everything would be all right, there was nothing left to say. Her experience with the Shadowkeeper hadn't produced new evidence.

"One more thing," she said. "In the back of my mind, I keep hearing a man's voice saying the curse. You know the one. 'Hear me, o goddesses. West, East, North, South.'"

"Did he change the words?"

"I don't know. It was like he was singing. Like a lullaby."

Before he allowed her family and friends back into her room, he reminded them that they should never blame the victim. Portia escaped with her life, and no serious physical damage was done. They should be grateful. And supportive. Then, he fled with Skylar.

On the way to Rogers's house, he reported Portia's story to her. "He used much the same model that worked with Phoebe, another reporter who was so hungry for a story that she disregarded her own safety."

"But Portia's assault is different," she said. "He attacked her during the day when there might have been witnesses. Might be a sign that he's becoming overconfident. And he didn't kill her. If you hadn't figured out that the column would be the next site, Portia would have been tied up all night and discovered in the morning when people came to work."

"According to the doctor, she had ketamine in her system, but she was never in real danger. It wasn't a lethal dose."

She shook her head. "Why was he singing the curse to her? It's a gruesome verse about scratching out eyes and muzzling his mouth. I think he's coming unglued."

Jake parked in the driveway behind Rogers's black sedan, making it impossible for him to leave. Together, he and Skylar walked to the front of the pleasant yellow house with white trim. Before he could knock, Rogers opened the door.

Scowling, he said, "This has got to stop, Armstrong."

"I don't know what the hell you're talking about."

"Harassment," he said. "Okay, maybe I wasn't completely forthcoming, but you people have to stop pestering me. There were cops watching my house all night. And somebody came by this morning and demanded a hair sample from Delilah, as if there are dozens of women with magenta hair running around town."

"May we come in?" Skylar asked.

He stepped aside and gestured for them to sit in the living room on the plaid sofa while he took the overstuffed chair facing the television. "Tell me why you need to test Delilah's hair."

"You admitted that you weren't forthcoming," Skylar said. "Please explain."

"Okay, I get it." He leaned back in his chair and lowered his heavy eyebrows in a squint. "If I tell you something, you'll tell me. *Quid pro quo.* Am I right?"

Without agreeing to anything, she said, "Let's start with why your black sedan was seen near Phoebe's apartment. Your excuse was something about stopping by to talk to her about newspaper business."

"Are you calling me a stalker?"

"If it wasn't you in the car, then who?"

His fists clenched, and he cursed. Jake could see that Rogers was barely holding himself together. "Can we move on? Please."

"Who was driving your car?" She continued, "Was it your son?"

Losing energy, his shoulders hunched. He rested his elbows on his knees and splayed his fingers, gesturing nervously. "I was trying to protect him. I haven't always been a good dad. When I found out he'd been taking my car, it seemed like a harmless little lie."

This conclusion had crossed Jake's mind, but he hadn't given it serious consideration. Not until now. That harmless lie had kept them from finding the Shadowkeeper. "You lied about your car to protect Bradley."

"I owe it to him for all the years I couldn't be with him.

Not that it was my choice to be an absent father. I didn't want the divorce and tried to fight his mother's move to Houston." He shook his head as if he could dislodge memories. "She was a beautiful woman. Still is. Didn't take her long to find a new husband in Texas."

"Knox," Skylar said. "The wealthy rancher. Did he abuse your son?"

For a moment, Rogers looked shocked. "How dare you—"

"Did he?"

"I never knew for sure. Didn't want to know. When Bradley came back to Astoria to attend school for part of the year, he had bruises. But he told me it was because he lived the outdoor life on the ranch. Riding horses and hiking and hunting. Damn, I hated that he was hunting. And he spouted a bunch of macho baloney about how a 'real' man is tough, aggressive and doesn't take sass. Especially not from womenfolk."

"How long has your son been back in town?" she asked.

With a groan, Rogers climbed out of his chair, too uncomfortable to sit, and paced toward the dining room. He didn't need to state the obvious. Bradley had been here before Phoebe's murder because he took his father's car to spy on her.

Jake asked, "Did Bradley meet Phoebe when he was in Houston?"

"Knew her and didn't like her. She dumped him." He held up his hand to stop their line of questioning. "*Quid pro quo.* Before I say anything else, there's something I want to know."

Jake nodded.

"It's about Delilah," Rogers said. "Why are you so concerned about her hair?"

"Magenta hairs were found in a car that crossed the bridge to Cape Disappointment on the night when Lucille was murdered."

"Whose car?"

"It belonged to another suspect." Jake worked the math

in his head. Quilling and Bradley were roughly the same age. They might have been in high school at the same time. By framing him, Bradley could have been hitting two birds with one stone, implicating Delilah and Quilling at the same time. "Do you know Alan Quilling?"

"Nice kid. He and Bradley were friends."

Or enemies. "Someone might have deliberately placed Delilah's hairs in Quilling's car, then used his vehicle to cross the bridge."

Rogers sank into a chair at the dining room table and fell forward, dropping his head into his arms. "I don't want to believe any of this. My son isn't a murderer."

Jake's phone vibrated in his pocket. The caller ID showed Pyro Pierce. When Jake answered, his former science teacher talked fast. "Have you seen Dagmar?"

"What's wrong?"

"She said she was going to investigate. Now I can't get ahold of her."

Jake had a bad feeling about where his cousin might be. Like mother, like daughter.

Chapter Twenty-Five

Skylar stepped onto the porch behind Jake. The fog had thickened. She could barely see the house across the street.

Jake switched his phone call to Speaker so she could hear the worry in Pierce's voice when he talked about Dagmar trying to find the Shadowkeeper. She hadn't said where she was headed but promised to stay in touch. "That was two hours ago," Pierce said. "She's not answering calls or texts."

"I'll help you find her," Jake promised.

When he disconnected the call, his indecision and tension were evident. He didn't want to leave Skylar unguarded but needed to track down his cousin and make sure she hadn't made an impulsive, risky move.

"Go," she said. "Find Dagmar."

"You and I need to stay together."

"I'm not letting Rogers off the hook. He still has questions to answer." Like telling them where to find Bradley. "I'll call Crawford and have him join me. He's at APD, ten minutes away from here."

He slipped his arm around her waist, pulled her close and planted a firm kiss on her mouth. "I'll be back."

She watched him disappear behind a curtain of fog when he went to his car. Back in the house, she stalked directly toward Rogers who sat stiffly at the dining room table. He'd used the few minutes of privacy to pull himself together. No more talk of *quid pro quo*. He'd made his decision. "I want my attorney."

"You have every right to contact your lawyer. I have only one question." She paused for emphasis. "Where is he?"

"I don't know."

She believed him. There was no point in badgering Rogers. All she could do was sit here at the dining room table and wait, figuring that sooner or later Bradley would contact his father again.

A heavy silence spread across the room and settled over them. Minutes ticked slowly by. Then, the back door slammed. The sound of cowboy boots thudded across the kitchen tiles, and Bradley appeared in the doorway to the dining room. He held a SIG Sauer 9mm Luger in his hand. "Nice to finally meet you, Special Agent Gambel. I think I'll call you Skylar. Or Sky. Or Honeybunch. Would you like that, Special Agent Honeybunch?"

She rose from her chair and took a long step to her left to put herself in a position where the dining room table wouldn't be in her way. Skylar had no intention of making this a shootout, even though she was probably faster and more accurate with a firearm, but she wanted to take him alive, which meant hand-to-hand combat. Instantly, she was ready. A warrior. Her mindset shifted. Her body went on high alert, prepared for battle by years and years of karate training.

"I'm curious." She reached into her pocket and activated the recording function. "Why did you wait for Jake to leave before making your presence known?"

"Have you seen the size of that guy? He's Sasquatch."

But I'm more vicious, little old me. She took a jab at his oversize ego. "Poor Bradley, you were scared."

"I was smart," he said with a sneer. "I tricked you and your boss and everybody in the Astoria Police Department. Losers, all of them."

In her mind, she measured the distance she needed to launch a flying kick at his gun hand. Her martial arts training made her fast, powerful and accurate. Once the gun was out of the way, she could easily take him down.

"This is my fault," Rogers said. He pushed back his chair and stood, planting himself between Skylar and Bradley, getting in the way of her plan. "I need to tell you that I'm sorry, son."

"Yeah, great. Who cares?"

"The first time the Lightkeeper killer came around, twenty years ago, and threatened us, I should have gone with you and your mother to Texas. But I chose to stay here and report on the story. I put my career above my family."

"Your career?" Bradley scoffed. "You're a small-time editor of a small-town newspaper. Don't pretend you're Rupert Murdoch."

"I lost you both," Rogers said. "You and your mom."

"Mom already had one foot out the door. You could never give her what she wanted. You'd never be as rich as Knox. Or the new husband—the French guy who took her to Paris."

"Did that cowboy hurt you? Were you abused?"

"Knox taught me how to be a man. How to take what I wanted and move on. We hunted. He taught me how to kill without regret. He was good for me."

He stuck out his scrawny chest. He was taller than Skylar had expected, probably six feet two inches in his cowboy boots. But he was neither imposing nor intimidating. His wild, curly black hair was similar to his father's. His dark eyes, nearly ebony, stared at her, unblinking like a snake. Though not the type of man who stood out in a crowd, he had the uncanny ability to capture and hold her attention.

He pressed the barrel of his SIG into his father's chest. "Take a seat, Dad. This isn't your show. Today is about me and Skylar. She's going to do everything I say, and so are you."

He held up his phone. The screen showed a picture of Dagmar from the waist up. She appeared to be sitting on the floor and leaning against a dark wall. Her wrists were fastened together with zip ties. A silver square of duct tape covered her mouth. Her eyes were closed.

"You drugged her." Skylar braced herself for action. "Tell me where she is."

"Settle down, Special Agent Honeybunch." Bradley tucked the phone into his pocket and pointed to the dining room chair. "Sit down, Dad. I'm not going to ask again."

His father obeyed. Before he could object, Bradley plunged a hypodermic needle into the back of his neck. "Go to sleep, old man. When you wake up, everybody is going to know that your son is a genius serial killer who outwitted the dumb cops and got away with murder. Damn right, it's your fault. They're going to blame you for being a bad father."

While he watched his father drift into unconsciousness, he spoke to Skylar. "If you want to see Dagmar alive again, you'll do exactly as I say."

"What if I don't?"

"In about an hour, it'll be high tide. Dagmar could be underwater. Do you want to take that risk? Isn't it your job to offer your own sweet FBI body as a substitute hostage?"

She didn't have much choice. If she delayed or went too slowly, Dagmar might suffer. Bradley might have rigged something to drown her at high tide. "I'll do what you want," she said. "Take me to her."

"Disarm yourself. The Glock and the piece in your ankle holster. Any knives or Tasers or sprays. Oh yes, and your phone. Can't have you calling your boyfriend."

She stacked her weapons on the table. When she pulled the lethal Ka-Bar knife from her vest, he whistled his appreciation. "By the way, if you fail to follow my instructions, you'll be punished. I need for you to be able to walk, so I won't injure your legs. I'll start with a bullet in your left hand."

He sounded like he'd enjoy hurting her. She asked, "Where are we going?"

"Venture a guess?"

"No more games," she said. "Just tell me."

"You're tired of losing to me." He tossed several zip ties onto the table. "Fasten his arms and ankles to the chair. Then slap duct tape over his mouth. By the way, we're going someplace cheesy."

Her first thought was Tillamook, where the world-famous cheese factory and creamery were located. She turned off the recording function on her phone and placed it on the table. "Someplace cheesy?"

"Leave the phone here," he said. "I don't want to be tracked by some GPS device."

When she'd finished securing Rogers to the chair, Bradley tossed her a set of car keys. "You'll drive Dad's car. I'll be in the passenger seat with my SIG."

Standing at the dining room table, she analyzed the situation. Bradley had the upper hand because he knew where Dagmar was and she didn't. He'd taken away her most effective weapons, but she'd managed to keep her switchblade pocketknife and was still wearing her bulletproof vest. Most important, she'd left her phone with the recorded conversation. When Jake came looking for her, he'd have a starting place. "I'm ready," she said with a confidence she didn't truly feel.

"You know," he said, "Dagmar is obsessed with her mother's murder. I only needed one text message to lure her to me."

Much as she hated to acknowledge his cleverness, she asked, "What was the text?"

"'Hear me, o goddesses. Meet me at the marina. The Shadowkeeper.'" He laughed. "She couldn't stay away."

Jake would hear the phone recording. She had to believe he'd find them.

Chapter Twenty-Six

When Jake couldn't reach Skylar by phone, he rushed back to Rogers's house with Pierce. The black sedan was gone. So was Skylar. They found Rogers in the dining room.

Pierce removed the duct tape from Rogers's mouth and used Skylar's Ka-Bar knife to cut the zip ties. When Rogers toppled forward, still unconscious, Pierce caught him. "We need to take care of this guy."

Using his phone, Jake contacted Chief Kim at APD and told her to send an ambulance and an officer to accompany Rogers to the hospital. Then he played the recording on Skylar's phone, listening for clues. Bradley told Skylar she'd need to walk a distance. He never actually described the threat to Dagmar, but Skylar said she looked drugged.

Worried, Pierce tried to make sense of what they'd heard. "The location is cheesy. That points to Tillamook."

"Too obvious?"

"Occam's razor," said the science teacher. "The most obvious solution is usually correct. We have to accept that Dagmar is in imminent danger of drowning at high tide. We have to find her."

"We'll find both of them." Regarding the weapons on the table, Jake cringed. "Skylar is totally disarmed. I never should have left her alone."

"All for the best, Sasquatch. Bradley had to find Skylar

so he could use Dagmar as a hostage. Where do we go next? The cheese factory?"

"The marina. *Jolly Rogers* is a boat the editor keeps there. Bradley had access to his father's car, so it stands to reason that he also has keys to the boat."

Pierce finished the train of thought. "He can use the boat to go to Tillamook."

Jake remembered the night they followed Rogers to the marina. He must have been looking for Bradley. Didn't tell them because he was still protecting his son. "We start there."

They handed off Rogers to the paramedics in the ambulance and instructed the officer accompanying him to ask questions about Skylar and Dagmar as soon as he was awake.

Outside, heavy fog obscured the trees and the rusted swing set. Though Jake knew the temperature was in the sixties, a damp cold penetrated his windbreaker and whistled down his spine. His fear expanded exponentially, bigger than when he engaged in firefights, faced IEDs and fought armed combatants in the marine corps. Skylar was being manipulated by a serial killer who wished her dead.

I can't lose her. In a few short days, she'd become everything to him.

Behind the steering wheel of his Explorer, he went in Reverse. Rogers's black sedan was no longer in the driveway. "Cheesy Tillamook. How can we narrow down the location?"

"Think outside the box," Pierce said. "There's Tillamook the town and the river and Tillamook Bay on the coast."

"And an Indigenous Salish tribe," he said. "What else?" *Think. Think. Think.*

Together, they said, "Terrible Tilly. A lighthouse."

Jake knew exactly what to do. He hit a speed-dial number on his phone.

SKYLAR HUDDLED ON the double bed in the belowdecks cabin of the *Jolly Rogers*. Dagmar sprawled beside her—still out cold but showing signs of coming around. Skylar had removed the duct tape from her mouth, making it easier to breathe, and it was encouraging to hear Dagmar cough.

The interior of the old trawler needed patching and painting, but the only way Dagmar could have drowned in here was if a torpedo had blasted through the hull.

Bradley led her to believe Dagmar was trapped in a cave or some other enclosure where high tide would put her under water. He'd lied, which shouldn't have come as a huge surprise. The man was, after all, a serial killer with a badly skewed moral compass. To him, a lie was nothing.

While he piloted the boat from the helm, she looked for ways she could take advantage in hand-to-hand combat. The small, belowdecks area favored the larger, heavier opponent—all he needed to do was pin her to the mattress, and she'd be helpless. Bradley had the edge unless she could get him outside where she had room to maneuver. When they arrived at their destination, she had the additional benefit of having her pocket switchblade which she would use to cut the zip ties fastening her wrists when the time was right. The element of surprise could not be overestimated.

She heard the rumble of the twin engines change rhythm and felt the boat slowing. It hadn't been a long ride from Astoria. Where were they?

Bradley swaggered into the cabin and leaned over Dagmar. "I see you took off the gag."

"She was choking." Ironic, since that might be his plan for her.

"Just as well. I'd like for her to be awake enough to walk up the path to the lighthouse. Between the two of us, we can guide her, but it'll be easier if she's mobile."

"Where are we?"

"Terrible Tilly. The most famous lighthouse on the Oregon coast."

She shrugged. "If you say so."

"I keep forgetting that you're not from this area." He actually smiled, and his knife-edge features softened. His enthusiasm about the next phase in his plan apparently gave him pleasure. "We've landed on a solitary rock about a mile offshore from the Tillamook River. It's isolated. And small with a surface slightly more than an acre. Over the constant roar of the wind and pounding surf, you can hear the cries of gulls and cormorants and sea lions."

"You like this place," she said.

"Terrible Tilly is always where I wanted the Oregon part of my story to end. Standing on an iconic symbol of loneliness, facing all the pressures nature could generate and coming out on top, unshakeable and dominant. It suits you to be here with me. Your last sight will be the harsh Pacific crashing through the fog, dragging you to your doom."

"What about Dagmar?"

"I don't really care about her. You're the one I want. The high-achieving FBI special agent. I always knew there would be three women. Phoebe the bitch would be the first to go as payback for her hubris—she used men, then threw them away. Not me, though. Lucille the songbird was less evil but equally blind, disregarding my advances, giggling and blabbing in that annoying Texas twang. Portia didn't fit. She was too young. But you, Special Agent Honeybunch, are the epitome of a woman who thinks she's better than everybody else."

Like your mother? "If you didn't care for the Texas accent, why did you stay there so long? Your dad would have welcomed you home."

"I don't want to be the son of a loser," Bradley said. "I have my own pride. My own accomplishments. Mom never understood. When she took off with Frenchie to live in Paris, I knew it was time for me to show her what I could do."

Skylar saw a classic pattern playing out. Bradley rejected his father for not living up to some impossible masculine ideal. And he felt abandoned by his mother who found one wealthy mate after another and dragged her son along behind her. Without caring for his needs. Without consulting him. *Without getting him into therapy.* Her second husband after Rogers was Knox, an abuser. Her marriage to the Parisian might have been the trigger for Bradley to take on the role of the Lightkeeper—a serial killer he blamed for destroying his family twenty years ago.

Somehow, Skylar had gotten caught up in his fantasies. Just at the moment when she discovered something special with Jake. Skylar wasn't going to give up. Not yet.

Bradley reached around her and shook Dagmar by the shoulder. "Wake up, you wicked witch. You need to come with me. Now."

Jake might have contacted the US Coast Guard unit based in Astoria. Or he could have arranged a ride to Terrible Tilly with the harbor patrol. The best course would be to take a helicopter. Landing a helo on that desolate rock would be safer than approaching by sea, and he got Chief Kim working on it. Even with a sanction from SSA Crawford of the FBI, the red tape would slow him down. He and Pierce needed to move fast, and Jake knew another way: Tucker's Tug Tours.

They boarded the brightly painted tugboat in Astoria and chugged south to the solid basalt rock a mile offshore— the home of the Terrible Tilly lighthouse. The location had never been very successful. The weather was too severe. In high tides and storms, waves crashed against the west-facing side and splashed plumes of white surf higher than the beam that shone across the sea from the two-story tower atop a larger house. Ferocious winds threw heavy stones against the tower. Workmen and lightkeepers had perished on the one-acre rock. And there were supposed to be ghosts. From the tours he'd led, Jake knew the history.

After Tilly lost functionality as a lighthouse, it sold as private property. From what Jake heard, Tilly was for sale again with an asking price in the millions.

He and Pierce clung to the railing at the front of the tugboat, watching for the rock to come into view through the fog.

"When this is over," Pierce said, "I'm going to ask Dagmar to marry me."

"Funny," Jake said. "I was thinking much the same thing. Not about Dagmar. But...you know what I'm saying."

"You've only known Skylar a few days."

"It's long enough."

He'd never been in love before. Not like this. He knew Skylar wasn't perfect. Her beautiful face and athletic body counted as a plus, but he'd heard people call her bossy or brusque. Others didn't like her sense of humor. And her thing with bridges needed to be faced and dealt with. But she was perfect for him.

The fog thinned for a moment, and he saw Tilly. He gave the signal to Tucker who was at the helm, and the old man honked the spunky foghorn. Once. Twice.

We're coming, Skylar. Hang on.

HER HEAD TURNED when she heard the sound of the horn. She'd heard that blast before when Two-Toes Tucker's tugboat ferried her across the Columbia. Jake was on his way!

"Keep moving," Bradley snarled. "This isn't a sightseeing tour."

Leading the way, she climbed the rocky stairs chiseled from the natural basalt while he helped Dagmar. Skylar had already taken advantage of her position where Bradley couldn't see what she was doing with her hands. She'd maneuvered the pocket switchblade out of her pocket and cut through the zip ties, freeing her hands. Then she'd hidden the knife in the sleeve of her jacket. She wouldn't try an attack until she was certain that Dagmar was safe.

Still feeling the effects of the drug, Dagmar appeared to be woozy and weak, barely to climb.

Finally, they entered the large house below the tower. Faint glimmers of light spilled through the boarded-up windows. The filth and the stench of guano from nesting seabirds nearly overcame her.

Bradley released his hold on Dagmar, and she stood in the semidarkness, weaving and unsteady on her feet. He gestured with his gun. "That way. Take the stairs. We're going to the roof."

"Dagmar can stay here," Skylar said. "It's me you want."

But Dagmar lurched toward the stairs. "Stinks in here."

Skylar inserted herself between Bradley and Dagmar, still not revealing that she'd escaped the bonds of her zip ties. She hadn't really been able to see the rooftop but hoped there would be enough room to make her move. First, she needed to disarm Bradley. Then they could square off and fight. Her years of karate training and the recent addition of Krav Maga made her a worthy opponent. Was it enough to handle Bradley?

Gulping down breaths of the relative freshness of the outdoors gave her hope. The rooftop below the tower provided a wide, flat surface nearly the size of a football field. Skylar believed she could work with this, especially when she saw the tugboat bobbing in the waves at the foot of the rock.

Bradley stepped up beside her. "They'll never get up here," he said. "I put in a lot of work making a place for my boat to dock. Tilly isn't accessible."

But as they watched, Jake peeled off his windbreaker, zipped his vest, climbed off the tugboat and dropped into the water. She took an involuntary step forward, terrified for him. That water had to be freezing cold.

Dagmar had broken away from them. She took a position, leaning against the tower and raising her wrists, still bound together, toward the heavens. In a husky voice, she shouted, "'Hear me, o goddesses, West, East, North, South…'"

Bradley gaped. "Does she think she can curse me?"

Skylar took advantage of his momentary distraction to lash out with her switchblade. She stabbed at his gun hand, slicing the sleeve of his jacket. He dropped the weapon.

Dagmar continued. "'Scratch out his eyes. Muzzle his mouth.'"

Skylar made a dive for the SIG, but Bradley managed to kick it out of reach. Her well-trained body assumed a lethal pose with her weight balanced and her arms in position to strike. Instead of slashing with her open palm, she unleashed a fury of kicks. Bradley was driven back, nearly to the edge of the roof.

"'Bind his arms,'" Dagmar wailed. "'Heed not his plea.'"

Looking over the edge, Skylar saw Jake charging up the stairs. There was another man behind him. Surely not Two-Toes.

Bradley had darted back toward the gun. She caught up to him just in time, throwing him off balance. He fell onto his back. Glared up at her with pure hatred in his eyes.

Dagmar finished her verse. "'Death to the Keeper. So mote it be.'"

Skylar picked up the gun and aimed at Bradley. "Stay down. I'll shoot your left hand first."

She didn't want to kill him. Yes, he was a serial murderer who had taken the promising lives of two young women. On some level, she felt sorry for him. Mostly, she thought, he'd make an outstanding subject for the psychologists to study. And wouldn't he love all those hours of talking about himself.

Dripping wet, Jake staggered onto the rooftop. He straightened his posture as he walked toward her. "I see you've got everything under control."

"Was there ever any doubt?" She heard the *thwap-thwap* of helicopter blades. "I'm so glad we're not going to have to walk down those stairs."

The other man stumbled onto the roof and went to Dagmar. Pierce embraced her and kissed her. Over the rumble of the aircraft, he yelled, "Marry me, Dagmar."

"Yes." She looped her arms around him.

"Show off," Jake said. He took a pair of soggy handcuffs from his vest pocket and ordered Bradley to roll onto his stomach. When he was cuffed, he returned to Skylar's side.

She lowered the gun and embraced him, even though the helicopter crew was watching. She'd shocked herself. Could be a consequence of nearly being killed. It was unlike her to make a public display of affection.

Even more unusual, she said, "I love you, Jake Armstrong."

"And I love you."

She beamed. "I know."

"In approximately one year, you'll marry me," he said. "During the annual Great Columbia Crossing when the Astoria-Meglar Bridge is open to the public. At the peak, we will exchange vows."

"And live happily ever after."

She could hardly wait.

* * * * *